Wil

TRICIA O'MALLEY

Wild Irish Rebel
Book 5 in the Mystic Cove Series

Cover Design: Alchemy Book Covers
Editor: Emily Nemchick

For my mother, Andrea, for always being the one to stand for me.

"There's nothing so bad that it couldn't be worse."

~Irish Proverb

Chapter One

STOP IT!" Morgan McKenzie awoke on a screech, her throat burning as she clawed at her chest, gasping for air. The beginning of a panic attack burned in her stomach and she struggled to orientate herself.

"Oh no." Morgan jerked her head up and tried to focus her mind away from her panic attack and on the more pressing issue at hand.

That issue being the entire contents of her small studio apartment levitating around her.

Including her bed.

"Okay, just breathe, focus," Morgan ordered herself, desperately trying to lower the objects that hovered around her. She didn't own much in this world and what she did was precious to her. If Morgan shattered her lamp because of a recurring nightmare that she had it would take her at least a week's worth of work to pay for another.

Morgan breathed a small sigh of relief as her bedside table and lamp settled back onto the ground. However, lowering her bed without creating a loud thump for her neighbors below was another thing, and she counted to ten in her head to force herself to concentrate before she timidly lowered the bed gently back onto the ground.

"Oh, this just has to stop," Morgan muttered to herself as she shoved out of bed and walked to the small kitchenette tucked in the corner.

The apartment was tiny and had just barely been within her budget, but Morgan didn't care. It was really nothing more than a large room tucked on the third floor of a small apartment building on the edge of town. But the worn wood floors and curved paned windows had appealed to Morgan and the high ceilings with exposed beams made the space seem larger than it was. With the help of her boss Aislinn, she'd been able to fit a double bed and loveseat, along with a table and two chairs, into the room. Prints of Aislinn's moody seascapes ranged across the brick wall, bringing color and movement to the room. Morgan had secretly delighted in buying a delicate sea-foam-green comforter for the bed with matching towels for the small bathroom tucked off the kitchen.

It wasn't much, but it was home.

Aside from her van, this was the first space that Morgan could call her own. After years of being unceremoniously moved from foster home to foster home, Morgan had a natural aversion to putting down roots. Until she'd come to Grace's Cove and had found herself able to build friendships for the first time in her life.

And found people who shared similar gifts to hers.

It hadn't been easy for her…growing up without a family, struggling to understand an otherworldly ability that would seemingly act on its own accord. It had gotten so bad that the nuns had periodically tried to exorcize her of demons.

Morgan shuddered as she measured out coffee for her French press.

Talk about instilling deep-rooted insecurities, she thought. Morgan hated the dreams that forced her to relive that time in her life. The nuns had been convinced that they were acting on God's behalf. Only Baird, Aislinn's husband and the resident psychiatrist, had shown her that being tied to a bed and prayed over for hours was really a form of child abuse.

Baird. Morgan breathed out a sigh of relief as she thought of her mild-mannered psychiatrist and friend. He had offered her sessions for free at the request of his wife, and her employer, Aislinn. Her eyes teared up just thinking about how much they had both helped her in such a short time. Morgan was quite certain that she would simply die if she ever disappointed them.

And it wasn't just Baird and Aislinn that had helped her, Morgan thought as she impatiently waited for her coffee to brew. Flynn had taken a chance on her by hiring her to work on his fishing boats with him. His wife Keelin was coming into her own as a healer and she'd been pushing Morgan to spend time with her grandmother, and the greatest healer in all of Ireland, Fiona. Morgan's scalp itched as she thought about meeting with Fiona. She'd spent so long trying to hide her extra abilities that going to Fiona seemed like ripping a bandage off of a wound. She just wasn't ready to tackle that step yet.

And then there was Cait and Shane. Cait was a bossy pub owner, now hugely pregnant, who had nosed her way into Morgan's life and began ordering her around like she'd known Morgan forever. Though Morgan put up a token fight now and then, she secretly couldn't help but love the fact that someone cared enough to boss her around. Cait's husband Shane had gotten her this apartment and Morgan was quite sure that he'd given her the family discount. A debt that she intended to repay with a free year of babysitting once their baby was born.

Morgan's mind circled back to Aislinn's gallery, Wild Soul. She'd taken a chance that day when she'd used her powers to stop a painting from falling from the wall. It had been such a beautiful piece that Morgan had reacted instinctively. Aislinn had witnessed Morgan using her power to save the painting and instead of running her out of town, she'd hired Morgan and had become her mentor.

Morgan didn't know whom to thank for the gratuitous turn of events in her life, but something had nudged her towards Grace's Cove. Finding a small town full of people who shared similar gifts to hers had been the best thing that had ever happened to her.

The scent of coffee teased Morgan's nose and pushed her out of her thoughts. Morgan sighed in relief as she reached up for her one and only mug, a rejected pottery experiment that Aislinn had deemed too ugly for sale. Morgan loved the overlapping cream and turquoise glaze and had insisted on taking it home with her. Drinking from it every morning was a reminder of how far she had come.

And just how much she had to lose.

Morgan's gaze tracked around the room, making sure that nothing had been broken during her nightmare. She'd yet to figure out how to control her power during her sleep, and most especially during her nightmares. It was one of the main reasons that she didn't date anyone and had never slept at a man's house.

She could only imagine a man's face if he were to awake to see a desk hovering above them. He'd run screaming into the night.

Morgan shook her head and took a sip of her coffee. "Just let it go," she ordered herself. These nightmares always made her feel melancholy and brought her right back to being tied to a bed while Father George screamed at her in Latin. She'd have to bring this up to Baird sometime.

Glancing at the clock, Morgan realized that she'd been lost in her thoughts for too long. She ducked into the bathroom and peered into the tiny mirror, grimacing at her reflection. Dark circles smudged eyes that couldn't decide if they were blue or green, and her skin looked pale. She pinched her cheeks for some color and pulled her long dark hair into a braid before wrapping it into a bun. Stripping, she stepped into the shower and washed quickly, reaching out to take large gulps of coffee from the mug that she had placed on the counter. She wished that she could stay under the warm stream for a while longer, massaging the knots in her neck from a night of fitful sleep. Instead, she dried off in a hurry, brushed her teeth, barely glancing in the mirror before snagging her coffee cup on the run.

Morgan rarely applied makeup. What was the point? She worked on a fishing boat and didn't date, so she found little need for it. Morgan dressed quickly, pulling a simple t-shirt and waterproof fishing overalls on and tucking her feet into rubber-soled shoes. With a last glance at the clock, she grabbed an apple and a peanut butter sandwich from the fridge and left her tiny apartment.

Morgan tried to walk softly down the worn wood steps that led to the front foyer of her apartment building. It was just shy of 4:30 in the morning and she suspected that the other tenants wouldn't take kindly to her waking them up at this hour.

The crisp morning air welcomed her as she stepped onto the street of small town Grace's Cove. Named for the stunning cove that was tucked into the cliffs outside the town, it was an accepted fact around town that Grace O'Malley, Ireland's infamous pirate queen, had chosen the cove as her final resting place.

And, in doing so, had protected the cove with powerful magick. Most of the residents of Grace's Cove wouldn't speak of the magick that was found inside the cove; instead, they steered far away from those enchanted waters, knowing that only harm could be found there. Thousands from around Ireland flocked to the town, thinking that they would be the ones to finally venture into the cove and find the reputed treasure that Grace had buried there. The government had finally put up signs warning of a powerful current and forbidding people to enter as a safety measure.

Too many lives had been lost there.

And, yet. The cove seemed to accept its own, Morgan thought as she hurried down the quiet street, only the bakery showing a dim light and movement. Houses and shops clustered together on cluttered roads that all led down to the harbor. It was common to find unique places tucked among the shops, like one place that operated as a hardware store during the day and as a small pub at night. People in Grace's Cove were nothing if not inventive.

And, not shy to capitalize on an opportunity. Just as many people came to Grace's Cove to catch a glimpse of the enchanted cove as they did to enjoy the quaint, small town that boasted stunning views of the water. Pubs, restaurants, and bed and breakfasts made a killing here in the summer.

It was the winter months that were the lean times. Morgan sniffed the air, happy to scent that the chill of winter was dispersing and the balm of spring was rolling in. Working on the fishing boat had been particularly grisly during the winter months, but Morgan had been determined to hack it, which in turn had won over the begrudging respect of the other members of Flynn's crew.

Reaching the docks, Morgan made her way down to Flynn's pier, where a smaller fishing boat was tied.

Today was a cove day then, Morgan thought and smiled happily.

Morgan was the only one that Flynn could take into the cove with him. It was the place where he found the best fish and lobsters to supply his restaurants across Ireland. Fish caught there claimed a high price.

It was an honor to be included on those trips, Morgan thought and raised a hand at Flynn as she came to the head of the boat.

"Cove day?"

"Aye," Flynn said.

Chapter Two

FLYNN STOOD AT the bow of the boat, coiling nets and dropping them in spots that would keep them from tangling together. Not for the first time, Morgan admired his darkly handsome looks, mentally congratulating Keelin on her excellent choice in men. Not only was Flynn ridiculously handsome, but he was also a good man and a solid employer. Morgan looked up to him like he was an older brother.

And she supposed that he was, in his own right. The legend said that all female members of Grace O'Malley's bloodline held a touch of something special. Which would make her and Keelin related in an odd sort of way. And, through that, Flynn was a brother of sorts. Morgan had been relieved to work that out in her head after meeting Keelin. She'd begun to worry that she was developing a bit of a crush on Flynn. Once she'd moved him into the family zone in her head, it had disappeared entirely.

The boat that Flynn used for fishing in the cove was low and sleek, the fiberglass sides painted a cheerful red. Inside, it held all of the modern amenities that a boat could want, including a small bathroom tucked below that Morgan was forever grateful for. It wasn't the first time that her being a female on an all-male fishing crew had caused some awkwardness.

Morgan hopped easily from the dock to the deck of the boat and moved to tuck her small bag with her food and apartment keys in a cubby beneath the steering wheel.

"Bait done?"

"Not yet," Flynn said and Morgan nodded and moved to the back of the boat where lobster pots were stacked. Though much of what they caught was through the nets, lobster from the cove fetched a premium price. Without fail, they always found the largest and healthiest lobsters there. It would be the first lobster catch of the season as they edged into late spring and Morgan suspected that the baskets they had laid a day ago would already be full.

A bucket of herring stood near the baskets and Morgan had zero hesitation about shoving her hands into the mushy wetness of dead fish. She hummed to herself as she worked, barely noticing when Flynn started the boat and pulled slowly away from the dock. She took her time baiting the baskets, making sure each piece was secure in the small mesh bag before moving on to the next. When finished, she leaned over the side of the boat, dipping her hands in the cold water to rinse the bits of fish from her fingers.

"Coffee's there," Flynn said, nodding to a thermos he had put next to the passenger seat.

"Thanks," Morgan said, moving to the front of the boat to stand by him.

This was her favorite part of the day. As the sun crept over the horizon of the still water of the harbor, shafts of light stretched across the water, slowly illuminating the brightly colored buildings of the village. One by one, lights began to pop on and the village awoke as the boat puttered out into deeper waters.

Because this was Flynn's smaller boat, he kept closer to the shoreline than he would have with his larger fishing vessels. Morgan found herself scanning the large cliffs that sprung from the water just outside the village, dominating the coastline with their impressive presence, and drawing thousands of tourists every summer. They were stunning in their command of space, but Morgan always felt a tug of sadness when she looked up at them. There was something raw and elemental about the cliffs, jutting out of the deep ocean water to put her humanness in perspective, she thought.

"How's the new place?" Flynn asked.

"Good, thanks. I'm so grateful that Shane set it up for me," Morgan said. Flynn knew that she had been living in her van and yet had never questioned her about it. Another reason that she loved working for him. The man knew when not to ask questions.

"Do you have everything that you need?"

"Aye, I do. I got a bed and Aislinn helped me to decorate. It's really a perfect space for me," Morgan said.

"Good, we all need a place of our own," Flynn said and left it at that.

Morgan silently agreed with him. She just hadn't realized it until she had gotten her apartment. A hole inside her had been filled the day that she signed the lease and for the first time in years, she looked towards her future with hope.

"Offering is up front," Flynn said quietly as they approached two large cliffs that ended in rocky points, for all the world looking like stony guards that protected the entrance to the cove. Morgan didn't have to ask what he meant. It was understood by those that were allowed to enter the cove that an offering must first be given in order to ensure their safety. Morgan didn't question it.

Morgan made her way to the bow of the boat and found the small mesh bag. Shifting it around she could see the glint of metal and some crystals. Flynn cut the engine and silence surrounded them as they drifted into the still waters of the cove. Her heart clenched – just for a moment – as it always did whenever they entered the cove. Whether people would admit it or not, there was powerful magick here. Morgan could feel the weight of it press against her skin as though she was passing through a thin veil of smoke. Steam drifted into the sky from the still waters of the cove and the cliffs hugged the water in an almost perfect half-circle. A sandy beach stretched at the base of the cliffs, looking for all the world like the perfect picnic spot. Instead, it lay empty, the waves lapping gently against the golden sand.

Morgan hefted the bag and spoke loudly, her words echoing back to her from the cliff walls. "We would like to offer you these gifts as a sign of our respect for your waters. We promise not to harm the cove, nor are we here for unworthy purposes." Morgan never repeated the same words when she entered the cove, but the intent was the same.

We mean no harm.

We respect these sacred waters.

With those words, she tossed the bag into the water and it disappeared into the depths with a soft little plop.

"Let's check the pots," Flynn said and Morgan pulled herself away from the front of the boat.

It was time for work.

Hours later, Morgan stretched her back while looking at the pile of baskets in the back of the boat. The baskets had been teeming with large lobsters when they'd pulled them from the water and Flynn had been delighted with the haul. All in all, it had been a peaceful, if not busy, day. Flynn and Morgan typically worked in silence, with Flynn humming along to the music from the small radio in the dash. Morgan didn't mind the physical labor as it left her alone with her thoughts.

And, lately, she'd been thinking a lot about the managerial position that Aislinn had been nudging her towards at the gallery.

It wasn't that she didn't want to take it – she'd do anything for Aislinn. It was just that the old insecurities that had plagued her since childhood had crept up, making her question her ability to do the job well. She'd rather not take the job than fail Aislinn in any way.

Reaching a decision, even though it made her a little sad, had her slumping down in the seat next to Flynn and letting out a small sigh.

Flynn cast her a quick glance. "How are things at the gallery?"

Morgan sliced a glance at him. "Sure and I could swear that Cait was the one with the mind-reading powers, not yourself," she said, smiling up at him.

Flynn raised an eyebrow at her and smiled. "Work on your mind?"

"Aye, Aislinn wants me to manage the store."

"Well, that's a wonderful opportunity. It will allow Aislinn more time to paint and it's clear you've an eye for what you're doing."

Morgan angled her head at Flynn as the shoreline whipped past them.

"How so?"

"And weren't you the one responsible for the fancy design at her showing? What about the way the shop's been rearranged or how Aislinn's now selling prints of her work around the world? Surely that wasn't all Aislinn's work?"

Morgan couldn't help but smile at his words.

"I suppose that I've had a bit of a hand in that," she said.

"I'd say. Listen, I love Aislinn but she isn't the most business-minded. Half the time she closes the gallery on a whim to go painting."

"Which I've put my foot down about," Morgan said firmly.

"See? You'll do just fine."

"I don't know," Morgan said softly, shrugging her shoulders.

"Are you worried about quitting this job?"

"I don't want to lose it or leave you hanging," Morgan said on a rush of words. "You took a chance on me when nobody else would and it means the world to me."

Flynn slowed the boat to a crawl and turned to look at her.

"I won't be upset if you take the job. You deserve it."

"But, what will you do about going into the cove? Nobody else can do that with you."

"I've been doing it for years prior to you coming here," Flynn pointed out gently.

"Well, what if we made the cove day on Mondays when the gallery is closed?"

"Yes, I could do that, set up the pots over the weekend and then come in with you on Mondays," Flynn agreed easily and Morgan felt her stomach turn a bit.

"Did I just take the job at the gallery?" she wondered out loud.

Flynn laughed and patted her shoulder before turning back to the wheel and punching the engine up a notch.

"Sure and it seems like you did," he called to her over the sound of the motor.

Morgan smiled at him but inside her stomach was doing flips.

"We'll see," she said and shut her mouth, mulling over her words as the boat zipped into harbor. The village was busy this late in the afternoon and it made her smile to see people bustling about their day, going from market to home. Groups of school children in their uniforms raced through the town, taunting and teasing each other. And the lights at Flynn's restaurant shone bright.

"You'll be taking this batch here?" Morgan asked, motioning from the lobsters to his restaurant.

"Aye, if we have too many, I'll dry-ice the lot of them and send them up to Galway," Flynn said with a nod.

Morgan nodded and hopped easily from the boat to the dock as Flynn brought the boat near. Grabbing the large rope at the front of the boat, she tied it quickly to the dock, securing it and running back to the end of the boat to tie up that side as well. Working fast, they transferred the lobsters quickly.

"Run those up for me while I clean up the boat," Flynn instructed.

Morgan glanced at the mess of the boat.

"You sure?"

"Aye," Flynn said and waved her away.

Morgan hefted the lobsters that were in two large buckets filled with seawater. Though she was slim, she wasn't weak. Even so, the weight of the buckets made her step carefully down the dock, worried that she would spill the lobsters out. As she reached the boardwalk that ran the length of the harbor, she turned to the right and began to make her way towards Flynn's restaurant.

"Need help?"

A voice like whiskey with a hint of sex called to her and Morgan immediately felt herself stiffen. Telling herself to calm down, she stopped and looked over her shoulder.

"Hey, Patrick." She smiled easily.

Patrick Kearney hustled down the boardwalk towards Morgan and her heart twisted a bit. A wide smile combined with stormy gray eyes and a head of dark hair was enough to cause any girl to stop and stare. The fact that he'd taken an interest in Morgan had done nothing to ease her nervousness around him. In fact, it made it worse. She fumbled with buckets as he drew near. Patrick smiled and bent and for a brief moment, Morgan thought he was going to kiss her. Instead he slipped his hands under the handles of both buckets and lifted them with ease from hers.

"I can do that," Morgan said stiffly, then wanted to kick herself for sounding ungrateful.

"I know you can; 'tis easier for me as I carry buckets of ice all day long," Patrick said easily and swung up the small hill towards Flynn's restaurant. Patrick was head bartender and part-time manager of Cait's pub. He could often be seen doing everything from pouring a pint to serving food. Morgan liked that about him. He didn't mind pulling up his sleeves and getting the job done – no matter what was needed.

Morgan supposed that she had the same style of work ethic as she never hesitated to put the extra bit of work in as needed.

"Sure and it was a grand day to be on the water," Patrick commented as she fell into step next to him.

"Aye, 'tis true. One of our first real balmy days. I'm looking forward to more like it," Morgan offered, grateful for the easy conversation.

"How was the cove?" Patrick asked.

Morgan stiffened and shot him a glance.

"Fine. How do you know we were there?"

Patrick motioned with a bucket. "Best lobster comes from the cove."

"Aye, they do," Morgan agreed and then left it at that. At Aislinn's art showing earlier this year, Morgan had been surprised to find out that Patrick knew about some of the extra special abilities that the other women had. She'd been amazed at his seemingly easy acceptance of the fact that his boss could read his mind. Morgan wondered if he would be as accepting if he knew that the person he wanted to date had more power than the lot of them combined.

I should ask her to dinner. Maybe this time she'll say yes, Patrick thought. Morgan grimaced and slammed down the walls in her mind. She wasn't as strong as Cait was with reading minds but a stray thought slipped through now and then.

Morgan wasn't sure if she was ready to go to dinner with Patrick. After a long day on the boat, she just wanted to go home, shower, and curl up with a book. Morgan valued her space and, unknown to anyone else, she was slowly studying used business books that she purchased when she could afford them. If she was going to take on this job at Aislinn's, Morgan was determined to make it a success.

"I can't wait to get home and put my feet up, it's sure been a long day," Morgan said quickly, hoping to stop Patrick in his tracks.

A quick flicker of disappointment crossed Patrick's face and then his friendly smile returned.

"What time are you on the water in the morning?"

"Typically we are out there by five in the morning," Morgan said and then laughed when Patrick gave a dramatic shudder. "Not all of us can stay up all night drinking pints with the locals," she joked.

"It's more than that," Patrick said stiffly and Morgan immediately felt bad.

"I was just joking," she said as they reached the back door of Flynn's restaurant.

"Aye, I know. Alright then, enjoy your early night," Patrick said and patted her shoulder gently before walking away. She watched him move with an easy grace that she envied. People shouted greetings to him as he walked towards the pub and he'd wave a hand or shout back. Everyone knew and loved Patrick.

Nobody knew her.

It was enough to have her turn away and smile distractedly at Flynn's chef as he came to the back door. It would be wise of her not to forget that Patrick was the town's golden boy and she was still a mysterious outcast. It was better for her not to get too close to him.

She'd learned long ago that forming bonds brought questions.

And Morgan wasn't prepared to answer any of them.

"Day's catch," Morgan said with a smile and the chef nodded and scooped the buckets from the stoop. A waft of air filled with the tantalizing smell of butter and garlic caused her stomach to growl and she wished that she could afford to eat at Flynn's restaurant.

Instead, Morgan tucked her hair behind her shoulder and headed for her little apartment, keeping her head down to avoid meeting the eyes of people on the street.

Chapter Three

PATRICK WATCHED MORGAN scurry up the road like a frightened mouse, her shoulders hunched and her eyes on the street in front of her. She missed the appreciative male gazes that lit upon her as well as the friendly smiles of the locals. The message was loud and clear – leave me alone.

He sighed and reached up to massage a knot in his neck. Ever since Morgan had come to town, Patrick had eyes for no other. There was just something about her that had hooked him immediately. The most obvious fact being that she was mind-numbingly gorgeous. Her slim body with moody eyes the color of the sea after a storm coupled with her shy demeanor made him want to dig beneath the surface to find out more about her.

And hadn't that gone well the last time he had tried?

Patrick groaned and made his way towards the pub as he flashed back to that night in Aislinn's courtyard when he had helped Morgan to carry some driftwood pieces to the gallery. The sun had been setting and it had cast a warm glow over her smooth skin, lighting up her eyes and drawing his gaze to her full lips. He'd felt compelled to lean down to kiss her.

He'd all but had a heart attack when she had screamed like he was hurting her. Patrick had jumped back, thinking there was a spider or something, when Baird and Aislinn had crashed through the gate. One look at Morgan had told him all he needed to know. The girl had been scared of him and Baird had quickly ushered Patrick away.

It had been a bitter pill to swallow, one that deeply offended his strong code of ethics. He'd kept his distance from her, but unfortunately, that had done little to tamp down the fire that kindled within him whenever Morgan was around.

Patrick pushed through the door of the pub, noting that Cait must already be here if the door was unlocked.

"Cait?"

"Over here." Her sharp voice called to him from the dining area. Her short hair and slim frame only made her huge belly that much more prominent. Cait turned with her hand on her back and gestured to the stage.

"Do you think that we need to paint that wall? Move the speakers around?"

Shane had warned him about this so Patrick stepped softly.

"We just painted it last year. It looks right nice now with that deep green."

Cait crossed her arms and studied the wall and then turned to glare at him.

"You think that this is just pregnancy hormones?"

Patrick raised his arms in defense. "I didn't say that!"

Cait tapped her head with one finger and then narrowed her eyes at him again.

"Listen, I know that women like to nest towards the end of their pregnancies. My sister was a mess. She re-did almost the whole house. Since this is like your home, I'm not surprised that you are looking to make some changes is all." Patrick hoped that his voice sounded as soothing as he could make it and was rewarded with a smile from Cait.

"Aye, you're right. I'm just itching to make changes. I guess that I'm just nervous about the baby."

"You know we'll all be here to help. He's going to have the best family."

"Or she," Cait said stubbornly and Patrick laughed.

"Well, the pool is running neck and neck for a boy or a girl."

"Let me see it," Cait demanded and Patrick held up his hands again.

"I can't do that. Who is to say that you won't try to sway the outcome?"

"Sure and you don't think that I can change the baby from a boy to a girl now, do you?" Cait raised an eyebrow at him.

"No, but it is also by day and time of birth so…you know." Patrick shrugged his shoulders.

"Trust me, Patrick, if I could make this baby come any faster then I would. She will come when she damn well pleases."

"You mean he, of course," Patrick said with a smile as he pulled a sheet of paper from a folder by the bar. Cait grabbed it from his hands and scanned it.

"You picked a boy, that's why you keep saying it is a he," Cait said with a sniff and then raised an eyebrow at him. "3:33 am?"

Patrick shrugged. "It's a lucky number."

Cait laughed and then paled when she scanned the last column.

"Sure and people don't think that I'll be waiting an extra three weeks to give birth?"

Patrick cleared his throat. "Erm, well, uh, they say that the first can go longer is all."

Cait turned steely eyes on Patrick.

"The baby will come by its due date and no longer. I simply won't allow it."

Patrick snatched the paper back from her.

"And that is why you aren't supposed to see this. You can skew the results."

Cait rolled her eyes and walked away, muttering to herself. Turning back, she looked at him again.

"What's up with you?"

Patrick stopped on his way to the long wood bar that wrapped around one side of the room.

"Me?"

"Aye, you seem sad."

Unused to discussing his feelings, Patrick just shrugged his shoulders and ducked under the pass-through and, out of habit, began cleaning a few empty glasses that were stacked near the washer.

Cait came closer and upon examining his face, pulled herself up onto a stool.

"Give, or I'm reading your mind," Cait ordered.

"Hey, stay out of there," Patrick grumbled.

Cait just raised an eyebrow.

"Alright, if you must know, it's Morgan."

"I could have told you that," Cait said.

"Well, why'd you ask then?" Patrick said angrily, wiping his hands with a bar towel.

"Because I want to hear what is bothering you about Morgan in this particular instance. You've been mooning after her for months."

Insulted, Patrick felt his cheeks flush.

"I have done no such thing," he said angrily.

"Well, I just meant that I know you've had an eye on her. Nobody else does, of course," Cait said quickly.

"She's just…she's so standoffish. I can barely get a chance to know her. I was going to ask her to dinner tonight when I saw her leaving Flynn's boat but it was like she read my mind and immediately cut me off." A thought occurred to Patrick and his head shot up as he glared at Cait.

"She can't read minds, can she?" he asked, accusation lacing his voice.

This time, it was Cait who held up her hands in defense.

"I certainly don't know that, now do I? I barely know the girl."

Patrick shot Cait another suspicious glance before bending over to check the contents of the cooler.

"It is like she is wearing a STOP sign on her," Patrick grumbled as he straightened. Cait had a look of sympathy on her face as she watched him.

"Be patient with her, Patrick. She's had a rough upbringing."

"So Baird has said. Yet nobody has bothered to tell me more."

Cait shrugged her shoulders and reached across the bar to pat his hand.

"It's not our story to tell."

Chapter Four

LATER THAT NIGHT, Morgan uncurled herself from the corduroy loveseat that hugged one small wall of her apartment. She stretched on her tiptoes, working out the aches in her neck and back from bending over a book for hours.

Aislinn had offered Morgan a manager position at Wild Soul Gallery just after her art show in Dublin. Though Morgan had been acting in that capacity for Aislinn for a while now, she'd been reluctant to officially accept the position. Aislinn bothered her about it on a weekly basis and Morgan knew that one of these days she would have to give her a formal answer.

Morgan found herself biting her thumbnail and pulled her hand from her mouth, silently lecturing herself. She knew why she was nervous about taking the job from

Aislinn. After years of being rejected from homes as a foster child, Morgan was terrified of letting anyone down.

Her sessions with Baird were slowly teaching her to have more confidence in herself and even he had told her that she was an excellent fit for the position.

It was just her own demons that she had to get past.

Sighing, she glanced back at the business book folded open on her small coffee table. Slowly, she was beginning to understand the finer nuances of a business budget, as well as the need for various marketing plans and the need for passive income streams. Helping Aislinn to begin selling prints of her work had been a boon for the business so far and one that eased some of the tension that Morgan had about taking the job.

She'd just completed the last of the business books that she had wanted to get through. Flynn had given her the go-ahead to start the job. Baird and Aislinn wanted her to take it and Morgan knew it would ease some of the load from their shoulders as they were busy decorating their new house and adjusting to life as a couple.

A little thrill of excitement slipped through her and for the first time in ages, Morgan laughed freely to herself and did a giddy little spin in her apartment.

Tomorrow, she was going to accept the job.

Chapter Five

MORGAN ENTERED THE courtyard tucked behind Wild Soul Gallery and smiled at the sight that greeted her. Aislinn must have had a painting session the night before because several canvases stood along the fence, drying in the soft light of the morning sun. Instead of Aislinn's usual turbulent seascapes, these paintings reflected the bright colors of village life. Morgan nodded her head in approval and made a note to have them made into small prints and postcards. They would be perfect for the upcoming tourist season.

Taking out her keys, she moved to the shop door only to find it slightly open. Pushing the worn wood door wide, she stepped inside to find Aislinn rinsing her brushes in the small kitchen at the back of the gallery. Her mass of curls was piled on top of her head and she glanced back at Morgan with an easy smile.

"Morning," she said.

"Good morning. Your paintings are beautiful. Please tell me that you aren't still up from working on them?" Morgan asked as she moved further into the shop to stand beside Aislinn.

"Aye, I am at that. But, I'll be off to bed soon. I just got a bug in me last night and it was the first real balmy night we've had in a while. I couldn't resist painting under the stars," Aislinn said and took down a small towel from the shelf above the sink to pat her brushes dry.

Morgan found her mouth going dry and she struggled for a moment as she tried to form the words that she wanted to say.

Aislinn turned and peered at her, a concerned look crossing her face.

"Okay, what are you scared for? I can read you a mile away," Aislinn said.

Morgan blew her breath out on a laugh. "I keep forgetting that I can't hide stuff from you and the other ladies," she said and shrugged her shoulders.

"Well, go on," Aislinn said, drying her hands on a small towel.

"If the offer still stands, I'd like to accept the position as manager of the gallery," Morgan said quickly and jumped when Aislinn let out a cheer and hugged her.

Her shoulders immediately stiffened when Aislinn wrapped her arms around her and Morgan tried to remember what Baird had taught her about returning easy affection. She wrapped her arms around Aislinn and squeezed back, knowing that this woman, with the big heart and generous soul, had saved her life.

Aislinn pulled back and studied Morgan's face.

"You're perfect for this job, you know that, right?"

Morgan just shrugged her shoulders and looked at Aislinn, surprised to feel tears prick her eyes. "I just, I don't want to let you down. I want you to feel comfortable with me managing your work and I want you to be proud of me, and what this gallery can become." Her words came out on a rush of breath, but Morgan was happy that she said them. She was working on opening up to people and Morgan knew that honesty with her emotions was something that would help her to form better bonds with others.

Aislinn's face softened and she patted Morgan's arm.

"Listen, Morgan, I may come across as carefree and head-in-the-clouds with my business, but despite the appearance, I am a hard worker and driven to succeed. I would never put someone at the helm of my business if I didn't trust them implicitly."

Aislinn's words emboldened her, but helpless not to, Morgan reached out and did a quick scan of Aislinn's mind and feelings. What she found there made her cry just a little harder.

Aislinn believed in her completely. Not only that, she loved Morgan.

"Get what you need?" Aislinn asked, knowing that Morgan had dipped into her personal space.

"Yes, I'm sorry, that was rude of me," Morgan said, wiping her eyes.

Aislinn smiled up at her.

"You've no reason to apologize. I understand why it is particularly hard for you to believe that someone wants you to stay – believes in you. But that is in your past now."

Morgan nodded, wiping her eyes again. Straightening, she smiled at Aislinn. "Thank you for the opportunity."

"Now, let's talk salary," Aislinn said and began outlining what she had in mind for Morgan. By the time she was finished, Morgan's mouth had dropped open and she grasped the side of the counter to keep the wave of dizziness that hit her from sending her stumbling back.

"You can't be serious," Morgan said. It was more money then she'd ever dreamed of making in her life. Granted, she knew that she lived a humble life and at best, lived paycheck to paycheck. This new salary would allow her to actually put some money away in a savings account.

"I never joke about money," Aislinn said.

"This will change my life. I won't feel like I will be constantly worried about making rent!" Morgan exclaimed.

"Aye, and maybe you can even move into a bigger place," Aislinn said and Morgan immediately sobered.

"No, I like my place just as it is. It is the first spot that I can call my own," Morgan admitted. Aislinn didn't say anything, only patted her arm in understanding.

"I'm off to sleep for the day. If Baird stops in, tell him I'm at the house and not to wake me up. Unless he plans to do something about it," Aislinn said with a wicked smile and slipped out of the back door.

Morgan stayed where she was for a moment, taking deep breaths and trying to process the benefits of her new role as manager. She'd never even considered a pay raise when she'd thought about taking the job and now Morgan was glad that she hadn't known about it. The amount of money she was now making would surely have put her off from ever accepting the job.

A feeling of pride slowly slipped through her. It was foreign to her, feeling proud of her accomplishments, and on a small laugh she wrapped her arms around herself and looked out at the gallery.

Today was the beginning of her new life, she decided.

Stepping into the gallery, she ran a critical eye over the room. When she'd first started working for Aislinn, Morgan had taken it upon herself to use her power to rearrange the shop. Feeling a little more confident in her ability to change things now, Morgan decided another makeover was needed.

First, she strolled through the racks of prints and towards the large windows that ran the length of the front room. They stretched from street level to ceiling height and offered passersby an unobstructed view of the artwork. When she'd first rearranged the gallery, she had done so with the intent of allowing the customer an easier browsing experience. Now, she wanted to do something to really draw the clientele in.

Morgan turned to the windows and snagged the cord that controlled the blinds. Without a second thought, she dropped the blinds to the floor so people walking by couldn't look in. Making sure that the closed sign was still up, she turned again, her hands on her hips.

"Alright then, let's start with moving the print racks back by the cash register," Morgan said out loud. "That way when a customer is ringing something up, they may make an impulse purchase. Plus, it will force them to walk through the gallery to get to the more affordable items."

With a nod, she glanced around one more time, ensuring that she was alone, and then moved the racks with her mind. They skidded across the room, just barely lifting from the floor, before coming to a rest in a neat row by the cash register. Tapping her finger on her lips, Morgan began to circle the room, now wide open from where the racks had once been. The wall above her was dominated with Aislinn's most expensive work and Morgan agreed with their placement. Leaving those untouched, she wandered towards the back room and looked at some of Aislinn's newer works.

"I wonder if I set them up so each has its own mini-space…" Morgan wondered out loud and then went to the storeroom. There, lining the walls, were close to thirty easels in various sizes.

"Perfect," Morgan said and walked out of the room, the easels following her in a neat row. Walking into the gallery, she directed each easel to a place, with the three largest positioned facing the window.

"Now, for the art," Morgan said and scanned the room, moving paintings of the Irish countryside, small town Grace's Cove, and seascapes to various points around the room. She stopped in front of a large oil painting of the cove.

"So it's you who has given me this power, is it?" Morgan murmured as she traced her finger down the edge of the painting. Aislinn had told her that all female descendants of Grace O'Malley had a touch of power, but Morgan knew little else. She knew that Aislinn wanted her to go to Fiona, the great healer, to learn more about her past. Morgan just wasn't sure if she was ready for it. It was almost as though she needed to get steady on her feet first before claiming a family history that she knew little about.

One that would give her an actual identity, she lectured herself as she lifted the painting and moved it towards the front of the shop.

It was funny, Morgan thought, that she was so reluctant to learn about her ancestry. Perhaps because she had been protecting herself for so long that she was scared to learn anything that connected her to her past. It was easier to move forward, never looking back.

Morgan settled the painting on the large easel in the middle and stood back. She sighed in pure envy of Aislinn's artistic prowess. She had painted the cove at sundown. The golden rays of the sun sliced across the sea-green water of the cove, illuminating the rock walls above the beach and casting shadows on the cliffs that hugged it. The painting was moody and beautiful at the same time; nobody who saw it would remain untouched. Morgan would be sad to see it go.

Making a note to purchase a print of this painting as her first purchase with her new salary, Morgan picked two other paintings to flank the seascape. One was a cheerful depiction of the colorful stores that lined the waterfront in downtown Grace's Cove and the other was a dreamy watercolor landscape that showcased the infamous Kerry Green pastures of Ireland.

Pleased with her work, Morgan stepped back and scanned the gallery. It looked edgy, like a funky artist's studio with a serious punch of talent. Anybody who walked past the window would stop for a second look. With a quick nod to herself, she pulled the cord to open the blinds and flipped the CLOSED sign to OPEN on the front door. Unlocking the door, she moved across the room and pulled the books from beneath the cash register, ready to run her numbers for the day.

Hours later, Morgan looked around her in dismay.

She'd never expected two tourist buses to unload in front of the shop that day. Her new window display had done more than she'd expected and not only had she sold the shop out of prints and postcards, but she'd also sold five paintings. Five! Morgan did a little dance as she raced across the room and locked the front door. This was their highest sales day in months and she couldn't wait to tell Aislinn the numbers. It would be enough money for Aislinn to finish the renovation of her apartment above the gallery into a studio.

Pleased with how her day had gone, Morgan finished up counting the money and placed everything in the safe in the storeroom. She was in a good mood, and contemplated going over to the pub for a pint. She rarely drank but sometimes it was fun to celebrate.

Undecided, Morgan swung outside and stopped in her tracks.

Chapter Six

PATRICK!" MORGAN EXCLAIMED, immediately feeling her shoulders tense up. Wary of him, she stood where she was.

"I brought you something to celebrate," Patrick said with an easy smile. He sat at the picnic table in the courtyard, legs stretched out in front of him, his muscular arms braced on the table. Morgan found herself drinking in the sight of him, all cool and casual, confident in his place in the world. A part of her desperately wanted to run over and jump on his lap, to tell him about her exciting day.

Instead she tilted her head at him and raised an eyebrow.

"Congratulations on what exactly?"

Patrick laughed and gestured to the ice bucket and glasses.

"On your new job! What else?"

"Word travels fast," Morgan murmured as she stepped closer to where Patrick sat.

"Small towns," Patrick said with a smile. "Plus, Baird stopped in for a late lunch and told me."

"Ah, yes, I'm quite excited," Morgan admitted and stood there stiffly, unsure of what to do.

"Come, have a drink. I've only seen you drink cider, and I've a lovely one here, made down at a little brewery on the Ring of Kerry," Patrick said easily and Morgan found herself warming to him.

"Well, I was considering stopping by the pub for a pint in celebration," she admitted.

"Ah, the lass does know how to lighten up once in a while," Patrick said, teasing her. Morgan was surprised to hear a laugh coming from her instead of her usual sarcastic response.

"I have my moments," she said and moved to sit on the other side of the table from Patrick. Sitting on the bench next to him would have been too close for comfort.

"Well, may I say that I'd like to be around for more of these moments?" Patrick said and popped the top on the bottle of cider, pouring honey-colored liquid into the glass and handing it to her across the table. A little shiver went through Morgan as her hand brushed Patrick's.

She hesitated before taking a sip, meeting his eyes over the rim of the glass.

"Thanks," she said.

"Sláinte " Patrick gestured and tapped her glass with his. Morgan gave a little trill of pleasure as the sweet liquid slipped down her throat.

"This is wonderful," she said.

"Isn't it just? I've got to talk to Cait about stocking it more," Patrick said.

Business, Morgan thought. She could talk business.

"So are you taking over for her once the baby comes?"

Patrick leaned forward, excitement crossing his face.

"Well, she's already made me part-time manager and then I'll be full-time when the baby comes. I like it. I can be more involved with inventory or running daily specials. I like to try out new things on the menu too," Patrick said.

"How did you end up working for Cait?" Morgan asked, keeping the conversation on him. It was an old habit of hers, leading the conversation so that people wouldn't ask too many questions about her past.

"Aye, well after school, I needed a job. I wanted to move out from my mum's and take a few years off to see if I wanted to go to uni or not," Patrick said.

"You're from around here then."

"We moved here from Kerry when I was ten. It was a little hard to adjust at first but I grew to love this town. People stand behind their own here."

Morgan sipped on her cider and pondered his words. She wondered why it felt like a threat to her. Would they run her out of town if they knew about her past?

"You?" Patrick asked.

"Ah, I don't think that I will go to uni. I'm not sure what I would major in," Morgan said, deliberately misreading his question. "What would you go for?"

Patrick leaned back and crossed his arms over his chest, looking out over the courtyard.

"I don't know at that. I've always had a hankering to build things…engineering has crossed my mind. Though the more that I am stepping into the managerial side of things at the pub, the business side of things is exciting to me."

"It is, isn't it? I've been reading all the business books that I can find and I really love it. The nuts and bolts of it, you know? Spreadsheets, budgets, marketing plans. It's great." Morgan stopped herself and glanced down at her glass, surprised to find it empty.

"Ah, so that is the book you ran home to the other night then," Patrick said.

Morgan shrugged her shoulders, a little embarrassed that she had revealed that part of herself. But, it had been the only way that she could learn about being a manager.

"It must have been a good read as you accepted the position then," Patrick said over her silence and filled her glass with the rest of the cider in the bottle.

Morgan was feeling a little warm and loose from the alcohol so she smiled up at Patrick.

She leaned forward and propped her head on her arms halfway across the table, her eyes wide with excitement.

"They're all good reads. I've absorbed so much. I knew that I wanted this job but I was scared to take it. Plus, I didn't want to let Flynn down. But we talked yesterday and he is fine with me coming in on my day off to help him out. He's got enough eager hands that he doesn't really need me. I suppose that he probably just gave me the job as a favor," Morgan admitted.

"You wouldn't have kept it if you couldn't hack it," Patrick said, leaning forward, bringing his face close to hers.

Morgan stilled as she suddenly realized that their faces were inches apart. With the sun beginning to set and the two of them standing in the courtyard, it immediately reminded her of the last time that they had been here and her poor reaction to his attempted kiss.

"Listen…" Morgan said.

Patrick cut her off.

"I'm going to kiss you," he said, meeting her eyes and giving her ample warning.

Plenty of time to say no.

Feeling almost hypnotized under his gaze, she nodded slowly.

Patrick leaned forward and she lost herself for a moment in his gray eyes, noticing the tiny flecks of green now that they were so close. Her eyes drifted closed just as he brushed his lips across hers.

A zing of heat shot through her and unable to help herself, she moaned softly as he deepened the kiss, sliding his lips across hers, nipping a bit at her full bottom lip. Morgan was lost in a sea of emotions, like all of her nerve endings had fired up at once.

This was her first kiss.

She wasn't sure why she had waited so long if it was as pleasurable as this. Patrick's hands cupped her face, tilting it so that he could continue to kiss her deeply, coaxing her to open her lips so he could slip his tongue in to tease hers.

Her eyes shot open as something bumped her arm.

A cold rush of panic shot through her as she realized that her glass and the ice bucket were hovering near her arm. Slamming her eyes closed, she poured herself into the kiss while desperately trying to concentrate on lowering the items carefully back to the table.

"Shit!" Morgan screeched as cold liquid splashed over her leg.

Patrick broke off and looked at her knocked-over glass in confusion.

"How did that happen?"

"I, um, must have bumped it," Morgan said, heat creeping up her cheeks. She wanted to bury her face in her hands. Chalk it up to another reason not to date, she thought. If this happened every time someone kissed her, she could only imagine what would happen if she took a man to bed with her. She'd have to bolt all of her furniture down.

Her eyes met Patrick's as he handed her a napkin to mop up the spilled cider.

"Sorry about that. It was really good cider," Morgan said weakly.

"No matter, I'm just sorry that you got wet," Patrick said. Morgan's eyes shot to Patrick's and her face felt like it was on fire.

Patrick let out a hearty laugh and then bent over, laughing even harder as he pounded his hand on the table.

"I didn't mean that to sound, um, dirty," he huffed out, struggling to breathe.

Morgan found herself laughing at him, surprised that she could relax around him after their kiss.

Patrick leaned back over the table, his face serious again.

"I liked kissing you. I like you. It's no secret that I'm very interested in you," he said softly, capturing her hand with his.

Morgan quickly pulled her hand away and continued to dab the napkin at the wet stain on her pants.

"Um, yes, I suppose that I know you're interested."

"So, can I take you to dinner?" Patrick asked.

"Um, well, it's just that, you see…I don't date," Morgan said, continuing to wipe her pants, refusing to meet his eyes.

"Ever?" Patrick's voice rose up on a high note at the end of his words.

"Well, um, no, I guess not," Morgan said sheepishly and finally met his eyes.

"And you're not willing to try?" Patrick asked, surprise etched on his face.

"I just...I don't know if I'm ready," Morgan said lamely, her hands flopping around in front of her.

"Why? What happened to you?" Patrick said fiercely and Morgan immediately felt her walls go up. She took a deep breath before answering, remembering Baird's advice to try to form bonds with people. She reached out with her mind and scanned Patrick's, finding nothing but concern and genuine interest there.

Still, she found that she wasn't quite ready to talk about her past.

"I'm just not looking to date right now. I really want to focus on my new job," Morgan said, side-stepping the question.

"What about friends, then?" Patrick asked.

Morgan tilted her head at him and raised an eyebrow.

"Friends?"

"Yes, friends. I'd like to be your friend," Patrick said, surprising her yet again with his agile mind and how quickly he changed subjects.

"You want us to be friends?" Morgan asked.

"Yes, friends. Like this...sharing a pint. Grabbing a bite to eat. Going for a hike," Patrick said as he packed the glasses back into the small cooler that he had brought with him.

"That sounds suspiciously like dating," Morgan said as Patrick rose from the bench.

"Not if I don't kiss you," he said easily over his shoulder and with that, he disappeared from the courtyard.

Morgan found her mouth gaping open and she closed it with a snap, before laughing softly to herself.

It looked like Patrick had won that round, she thought.

Smiling, she traced her fingertips over her lips. Her first real kiss…and aside from her cider floating in the air, nothing traumatic had happened.

Morgan considered that a win on her behalf.

Chapter Seven

MORGAN PULLED NERVOUSLY at crease in her pants. Though she still resolutely went to her free sessions with Baird, it had yet to get any easier to open up about her feelings. Last night, she'd barely been able to sleep – between the excitement of accepting the job with Aislinn and her first kiss, she'd been all but bouncing off the walls of her small apartment.

"You had a smashing first day on the job," Baird said, smiling at her, and Aislinn felt a little wave of relief go through her. He was opening with an easy topic. She leaned back against the couch and pulled a pillow onto her lap like she usually did.

Protection.

"Well, it was sheer luck that those buses unloaded in front of the store," Aislinn said, downplaying her role in the sales.

Baird tilted his head at her and pushed his glasses back up his nose. Aislinn concealed a small sigh as she admired his good looks. It was something about the glasses, she thought. It just pushed him over the edge into sexy. Aislinn was a lucky woman.

"And I suppose it was someone else who managed long lines out of the store and carefully rung everyone up? And it was someone else who rearranged the gallery to look like an elite artist's studio?"

Morgan shrugged her shoulders and fought to keep a shy grin off her face.

"Yes, I suppose that I did all that."

"You should be proud of yourself, Morgan," Baird said, "We certainly are."

Morgan shrugged again and looked around the room, taking in Aislinn's moody landscapes on the walls.

"I'm trying to get better at being proud of myself," Morgan admitted.

"Why do you think that is hard for you? To praise yourself? To acknowledge that you've done a good job?"

Morgan shrugged again.

"I don't know. I suppose it seems boastful."

"Being proud of doing a good job and being arrogant are two different things," Baird said. "There's something deeper there. What is it?"

Morgan was surprised to feel sadness well up inside of her and a sheen of tears crossed her vision. She supposed that she shouldn't be surprised as she almost always ended up crying in sessions with Baird.

"I guess…I guess I just feel like I don't deserve it."

"And why is that?"

"Because nobody ever wanted me. I was never good enough."

"Ah," Baird said and leaned back, crossing his legs as he studied her. "So, just because you weren't the right fit for some foster homes means that you never deserve to shine? That you should always feel like you aren't good enough even when you clearly did a fantastic job?"

"I guess it's weird when you say it like that," Morgan said, reaching for a tissue to dab at her eyes. She was glad that she didn't wear makeup as it would be running all over her face at this point.

"See, the thing is, from where I'm sitting, I see an incredibly beautiful and wildly talented young woman. I want you to start working on self-affirmations."

Morgan scrunched up her nose at Baird.

He laughed at her. "Just give it a chance. I need you to praise yourself for one good thing that you do a day. And, just for a moment, allow yourself to feel the pleasure that comes with doing a good job or whatever it may be. Don't ask yourself if you deserve it or are good enough, just step back for a moment and praise yourself."

"So give myself a pep talk?"

"Something like that. You need to allow yourself to feel how positive thoughts about yourself will affect who you are and how you react to people."

Morgan cleared her throat and looked away. "Speaking of that..."

"Yes?"

"I, um, you know...talking about reacting to people," Morgan stuttered.

"Just spit it out, Morgan." Baird smiled easily at her.

"Patrick kissed me. And it was great. Until I spilled a pint all over myself," Morgan said in a rush of words. Just thinking about it again had her heart hammering in her chest and sweat breaking out across her back. It had been glorious and embarrassing all in the same moment.

"How did you spill the pint?"

"Um, that's one of those things that uh..." Morgan made a swirly motion with her finger and pointed at her head.

"Something with your ability?"

Baird knew all about Morgan's abilities. Probably more than any of the women in town knew. He'd promised her client confidentiality and from what Morgan could see in his mind so far, he'd never broken it. Not to mention she'd given him quite the display a few months back when in a fit of anger she'd made a glass rise and dump water all over his head.

"Well, so, the only time this kind of stuff happens is when I am dreaming," Morgan began and Baird stopped her.

"Did you have a bad dream?"

"Aye, the other night, it's fine." Morgan shrugged it off.

"Tell me what happens during the dreams."

"I…I am back in the bed that the nuns tied me to. I see their faces swirling above me in a circle, their voices chanting in Latin, candlelight flickering. It's me but it's not me. When I wake up, pretty much everything in the room that isn't attached to the floor is hovering in the air. I have to work pretty hard to calm myself down and lower the furniture quietly."

Baird swore under his breath which coaxed a smile from Morgan. It was one of the things that she always liked about him. He seemed relatable and not some sort of stuffy doctor type.

"You know that this was child abuse. What they did was horribly wrong," Baird said.

"Aye, I know."

"You'll need to find a way to take their power away," Baird said simply and Morgan's eyes shot up to meet his.

"I never thought of it like that."

"It's true. They have power over you. Even from miles away and years ago. We'll need to think up something that we can do…some sort of ritual to allow you to release the power they have over you." Baird leaned back and watched Morgan. "You know, Fiona would be perfect for this."

Morgan looked determinedly over his head.

"Not ready for that?"

"I don't know."

"Tell me about the pint," Baird said, swiftly changing subjects.

"Oh, so we were sitting in the courtyard behind the gallery. He'd surprised me with a pint because he heard about my job."

"Nice of him," Baird observed.

"It was," Morgan agreed, "and, for the first time, I was able to relax around him. We have some stuff in common what with managing businesses and whatnot."

"Go on." Baird gestured with his hand.

"Well, we were talking and I just kind of leaned over the table and he told me that he was going to kiss me. I think he was a little worried about what had happened the last time, so he gave me fair warning. I didn't stop him." Morgan blushed as she thought about his lips on her and how her body had seemed to burn from within. "I liked it. A lot. It was my first kiss," she whispered.

"I'm not surprised about that," Baird commented and Morgan raised an eyebrow at him.

"How come?" Morgan demanded.

"Ah, well, you are fairly standoffish. It would be tough for any guy to break down that barrier. It has nothing to do with your looks or personality though. You just put a big "back off" sign up."

"I suppose that I do," Morgan said.

"So? The pint?"

"Ah, yes, we were kissing and I felt the pint bump my arm. I opened my eyes to see it and the ice bucket floating in the air! Thank God, Patrick's eyes were closed. I tried my hardest to lower them both but I didn't do too well with the pint."

Baird laughed.

"Sorry, it isn't funny but it is."

Morgan smiled at him, finally able to laugh at herself. "It is kind of funny."

"I think that you need to learn to control your powers when you are distracted. Have you had any training in that or any idea how to do so?" Baird asked.

Morgan just shook her head at Baird. "None."

"I know you don't want to hear this…" he began.

"Fiona," Morgan said on a sigh.

"Bingo."

"Maybe I'll drive out there after work or something," Morgan agreed. Though she knew that she was just saying that to placate Baird. Morgan had only met Fiona on a few occasions and the healer had looked at her like she knew all of Morgan's secrets.

"How did you leave things with Patrick?" Baird asked.

Morgan slammed her fist onto her leg and looked at Baird, her eyebrows raised.

"He wants to be friends!" Morgan said, indignation lacing her voice.

"Does he now?"

Morgan felt herself nibbling on her lower lip as consternation filled her. "I told him that I didn't date and he just…was fine with it. Said he'd be my friend then." She crossed her legs to keep her foot from tapping the floor.

"Friends are good to have," Baird said.

Morgan rolled her eyes at him. "Either he is interested in me or he isn't. There is no in between."

"But there can be," Baird said with a slow smile. "The best types of relationships start from friendships."

"I don't know if I can be in a relationship," Morgan admitted softly and was surprised to feel a soft yearning fill her. She'd been so used to not forming bonds and not having a home, that having a healthy, normal relationship had never really seemed like an option for her. It was almost too much at once.

"You can. Be patient with yourself, you don't need to figure this out today. It takes time," Baird said gently.

Time, Morgan thought. For once in her life she had time to stay in one place and figure her life out. A smile slipped across her lips and she looked up at Baird, hope filling her heart.

"Then time is what I'll take."

Chapter Eight

MORGAN FOUND HERSELF laughing freely with a local who had wandered into the gallery later that day. Her early morning session with Baird had done something to loosen some of the constant tension that she carried around with her. It was almost like she could step a little lighter and not take things so seriously.

"You're a lovely girl, now where is it you come from again?" A softly rounded woman with smiling blue eyes leaned casually on the counter. Instead of brushing off the question, Morgan took a deep breath and smiled into the woman's friendly eyes.

"By way of Killarney," she said easily, not bothering to expand.

"Ah, lovely town. What brings you to Grace's Cove?"

Morgan thought about how to answer that as she wrapped up the prints that the woman was sending to her niece in the States.

"Well, just look at it here. It's hard not to fall in love with this town," Morgan said, hoping that the woman accepted her answer.

Her smiled widened and she nodded at Morgan. "Quite right, you are. Well, we're happy to have you. You've certainly done a wonderful job with the gallery. You should come to the pub more, we'd love to see you out."

Morgan made a noncommittal noise while silently congratulating herself on carrying on a successful conversation with a local. It wasn't so hard after all. Though she knew from experience that deeper questions always followed. For now, she was happy to make a connection and hoped that it would improve her reputation around town. It was obvious that people were curious about her past and when they couldn't uncover details, the rumor mill typically started working.

"See you at the pub tonight?"

"I'll try my best," Morgan said with a wave and blew out a breath of air as the door closed after her inquisitive customer.

"Okay, back to business," Morgan murmured and went to the computer to check the gallery's online orders. "Wow," Morgan said as she scanned the list. Checking her inventory sheet, she immediately updated any listings that would need to be backordered so as not to upset any customers and then moved to her prints file.

Pulling out the first one, she smiled at the picture of the cove where both the setting sun and the moon rising could be seen together. It was one of their most popular prints and Morgan knew that Keelin had the original over the mantle in her home. She carefully slid the print into the custom-sized envelope and then wrapped a twine strand around it in a bow, pressing a small dried flower to the middle along with the card of the gallery. She added a handwritten thank you on the back of the card. It was a small touch that Morgan added and she smiled down at it, knowing that their clients would appreciate the extra personal touch.

Humming to herself, she continued to work her way through the list and jumped when the tinkle of the little bell over the door surprised her from her reverie.

"Patrick!"

She was surprised by how excited she was to see him. Typically seeing Patrick just made her nervous but something had shifted for her the other day. Not to mention Baird's comment about being patient with herself to help her to relieve a little of the pressure.

"Hi, Morgan. I was just leaving the coffee shop and thought that I would bring you a tea."

Morgan raised an eyebrow at the takeaway cup he held in his hand. A t-shirt with Gallagher's Pub emblazoned across it hugged his muscular chest and his hair looked like the wind had tousled it a bit. It shouldn't have been as sexy as it was, and yet… Morgan felt a little tug low in her belly.

"That's quite kind of you. Something that friends do for each other, is it?" Morgan raised an eyebrow at him and crossed her arms over her chest.

A raspy laugh fell from his lips and she found herself smiling at Patrick as he shrugged his shoulders.

"Sure and can't I bring a friend a cup of tea?" he asked, returning her raised eyebrow with one of his own.

"You can," Morgan said, backing down. She reached out to grab the tea from him and gasped as little shivers of sensation slipped up her arm when her hand brushed across his.

"Too hot?" Patrick said, his voice heavy with meaning.

Morgan found herself staring into his eyes, her mind drawing a complete blank, as warmth filled her. She licked her suddenly dry lips and tried to think of something to say.

"Dear God, Morgan, if you keep licking your lips and looking at me with those big eyes, I'm going to take you upstairs and show you something really hot."

Morgan felt the blood rush from her face and a trickle of panic fill her. Right along with a wave of lust that slammed into her gut. Maybe going upstairs wouldn't be a bad idea after all.

Patrick's mouth dropped open.

"You're actually considering it," he said and moved in quickly, putting the tea on the counter behind her and caging her in with his arms. Morgan gulped as she felt the press of the hard counter into her back, and the hard length of Patrick on her front.

"I…I," she stuttered, unable to look away from his face.

"I'm going to kiss you again," Patrick said, warning her in advance.

Morgan could only nod. It was what she secretly wanted. She'd replayed the kiss from the other night several times, each time making her feel warm and lovely inside. She'd be lying if she said that she didn't want another taste. Praying that everything in the shop didn't go flying off the walls, Morgan closed her eyes as Patrick's lips brushed softly over hers.

The taste of him was sweet, mixed with something darker, a promise to be remembered, a wish to be given. Morgan moaned slightly as she pressed into Patrick, running her hands up his hard chest, allowing him to slip his tongue between her lips. A wave of lust washed through her, so dizzying in its promise that she stumbled against him. Patrick wrapped his arms around her, pulling her closer until she melded to every inch of him.

"Whoops," Aislinn said softly from behind them and Morgan jumped back, tears immediately pricking her eyes, anger and embarrassment slamming into her. Needing an outlet, she turned on Patrick.

"You shouldn't have done this at my work," Morgan seethed at Patrick, and Patrick raised his hands, backing up a step.

"Hey, Morgan, it's fine," Aislinn said immediately, reading Morgan's feelings.

Morgan swiped at her eyes angrily and turned to Aislinn.

"No, it's not. You've put your trust in me and I violated that by allowing this to happen here. I'm so sorry, Aislinn." Her lips trembled as she looked at her employer.

"It's not like I found you stealing from the cash register, Morgan. Trust me, I've done way worse here. Hey, Patrick," Aislinn said, giving Patrick an easy smile, turning her head between the two.

"Aislinn," Patrick said stiffly, his eyes on Morgan.

Morgan turned to him, not meeting his eyes. Why couldn't he see that this was a big deal?

"Please leave, and don't put my job in jeopardy again," Morgan said stiffly. She couldn't meet his eyes, knowing that she was hurting him, but unable to back down. She could read it all over Patrick, from the emotions he was projecting to taking a dip into his brain where he struggled to understand how someone so warm had gone so cold.

"Morgan, that's unnecessary. This isn't a high-level government job. Ease up on the guy, would ya?" Aislinn ordered and Morgan felt shame creep through her.

"I'm sorry, it's just that this job is really important to me," Morgan said softly.

"And I've said you won't be losing it, haven't I?" Aislinn said sternly.

Morgan nodded and finally faced Patrick.

"Sorry," she said softly.

"No problem," Patrick said. "I hope you enjoy the tea." With a brisk nod for Aislinn, he made his way from the store, embarrassment wrapped tightly around him. Morgan wanted to cry even more.

"Hey, are you okay? What was that all about?" Aislinn moved forward and ran her hand down Morgan's arm. Morgan stifled her impulse to drop her head onto Aislinn's shoulder and lean in for a hug.

"I just, I don't know. I didn't expect him to be here, okay? He surprised me with a cup of tea. We were supposed to just be friends," Morgan said, anger making her words come out in staccato jerks.

"Okay…"Aislinn said, her eyes tracking across Morgan's face.

"And, he just, he kissed me. Here, at my work. And my boss walked in. That's just…that's *bad.* If I lose this job and have to start over…I'd lose my apartment." Morgan's hands flew around her face as she punctuated each point, her breath coming fast, and panic winding its way around her lungs. She tried to calm herself down, knowing that paintings could start levitating any minute. "I need to step outside," she said and pushed past Aislinn to the back door.

Outside, the afternoon sun filtered through a low cloud cover, casting a warm glow across the cozy courtyard. Morgan leaned against the back wall of the gallery, feeling the warmth from the stones seep into her back.

"You didn't have to leave," Aislinn said from the door.

"I was afraid paintings could go flying," Morgan said, her eyes closed as she counted to a twenty in her head and let the warmth of the sun seep into her.

"Ah, okay."

"Which is another reason that I shouldn't have let him kiss me in there. Anything could have happened to the paintings," Morgan said, keeping her eyes closed.

"How so?"

"It appears that I'm unable to control that particular ability of mine when I am being kissed," Morgan said stiffly. The sun really did feel good and was doing wonders to soothe her.

"And you know this how?" Aislinn asked, knowing full well Morgan's history and her lack of kissing partners in the past.

"Patrick kissed me the other night. And my pint levitated and dumped all over my lap," Morgan said morosely, rubbing her hands up her arms.

A snort from Aislinn popped Morgan's eyes open and she turned to glare at her boss.

Aislinn slapped her hand over her mouth, but the riot of curls shaking around her head gave away her laughter. Morgan narrowed her eyes at her boss.

"You think this is funny?"

"Oh, God, yes. I'm so sorry, but yes, I do," Aislinn wheezed, another undignified snort coming from her pretty nose.

Morgan found herself relaxing. There was something about Aislinn's laughter that whispered of Morgan taking herself too seriously. She said as much to Aislinn.

"Oh, Morgan, I know that our abilities are a huge deal. Truly, I get it. But, sometimes you just have to laugh at the awkward moments," Aislinn said. She came to lean against the wall next to Morgan, a smile still on her face.

"It was my first kiss," Morgan said stiffly.

"I know, I know. And, I know how you feel about it since your incident in the past," Aislinn said.

The incident she spoke of was something that Morgan didn't care to remember. It had happened at the last foster home she'd been staying in. Things had actually been going along quite well and Morgan thought that she would be able to stay there until she finished school and maybe went on to university. Unfortunately, she'd developed a desperate crush on their oldest son, a year older than her at school. He must have discovered her diary because one day he had snuck her outside of school. Morgan rolled her eyes as she thought about how stupid she'd been. Here she'd thought he was going to kiss her. Instead, as soon as she'd closed her eyes, he'd pulled her skirt down in front of a yard full of other kids. It was stupid and immature, but the other kids' jeers and taunting had left a mark on her. Morgan had packed up her bag and left that night, hitting the road. It was the final straw in a life full of insults. She'd made it on her own ever since.

"You know then why this job is so important to me," Morgan said.

"I know. But you can't always live like you are on the edge. Just because everyone in your past was awful to you, doesn't mean that everyone in your future will be."

"I like it here. I want to stay," Morgan whispered.

"We want you to stay. Trust me, you're doing a fantastic job. A kiss from Patrick at the store is not going to ruin that for you," Aislinn said and squeezed her arm. "Now, let's get back in there and finish those orders."

"Yes, ma'am," Morgan said, feeling lighter. She stopped at the back door and looked up at Aislinn in the back hallway.

"I owe him an apology, don't I?"

"He's a good guy," Aislinn said softly before going into the gallery. Morgan's shoulders slumped as she thought about how she would apologize to Patrick. She hated emotional stuff, which is why she strayed away from relationships. Feelings get hurt, things get sticky. Best to keep it to the friends path, then. Satisfied with her decision, Morgan pushed Patrick from her mind and went to work.

Chapter Nine

SURE, AND IT HADN'T been that big of a deal, had it? Patrick wiped down the bar again, grumbling as he worked at a particularly sticky patch. It wasn't like Aislinn was going to fire the best thing that had happened to the gallery. Patrick shot a stormy glare at a regular who requested another pint.

"I'll get to it when I get to it," he said stiffly and then cursed himself as the regular's smile fell from his face.

"I've got you," Cait called and Patrick felt his back go up as his 8-months-pregnant boss eased under the pass-through of the bar and began to build a pint for the regular, chatting easily about the weather all the while. Cait shot Patrick a glare and Patrick returned it with his own.

"I'll be in the stockroom," he said, slipping past her and ducking under the pass-through. It was still early enough in the day that she could handle the few customers that ranged along the worn wood bar. Patrick would take his temper out with some manual labor.

An hour later, he surveyed his work. Not only had he unloaded all of the new inventory, but he'd reorganized the entire set of liquor shelves by type of liquor, and then in alphabetical order in their sections. With a nod, he turned to leave and jumped to see his pregnant boss standing in the doorway, her arms folded across her impressive belly.

"You work your mad off yet?" Cait asked, shooting him a glare.

"I'm fine," Patrick said, meeting her gaze.

Cait sighed and rubbed her belly, and Patrick immediately felt guilty for leaving her to tend bar.

"Let's get you off your feet. I'm sorry," Patrick said.

Cait waved him away.

"I'm fine. Though I'm happy with the organizing you've done in here, I've rarely seen you so upset. What gives?"

Patrick folded his arms across his chest and debated how much to tell Cait. Though he knew she could read his mind, he wasn't sure how much of his situation he should tell her or how embarrassed Morgan would be if she knew that he was repeating stuff back to Cait.

Cait sighed. "I know it's about Morgan. I'll hear it one way or the other, so you might as well tell me."

"I stopped by the gallery today to bring her a tea. I kissed her. Aislinn walked in. Morgan freaked out at me for putting her job in jeopardy. I left. End of story." Patrick bit out the words as he clenched his fists, furious at himself for not sticking to the "just friends" agreement.

"Oh, well then," Cait said.

"I mean…like Aislinn would fire her. Come on," Patrick scoffed and paced the small room. He was beginning to wonder why he was even mooning after this girl. At this rate, it would take him years to get close to her.

"No, I don't suppose that Aislinn would at that," Cait agreed. "Just…be gentle with her, okay? She's not like your regular girls."

Patrick rounded on her.

"So everyone keeps saying and yet nobody will really tell me what's so different about her," Patrick seethed.

"She had a rough upbringing. You know this. It has to come from her, not us. Now either you decide to be patient with her and stick it out, or get over her, move on, and get the heck out of my storeroom," Cait ordered and turned, slamming the door, leaving him alone in the storeroom.

Patrick threw up his hands. "I've had it with moody women today," he shouted through the door.

"I heard that!" Cait called to him and Patrick winced.

Chapter Ten

"Why don't we call it a day?" Aislinn said a little while later.

"But, we still have another two hours..." Morgan protested.

"I know. I'd like to get some painting done though and I think that you could use the break. You know, Fiona mentioned needing some help with a few tonics that she was making," Aislinn said, keeping her eyes trained on the prints that she was stacking by the window.

"You too?" Morgan asked. What was with everyone pushing her to go see Fiona?

"It's a nice day for a drive," Aislinn said easily.

"I can't just drive up there and surprise her," Morgan protested, feeling like her last excuse for hiding from Fiona was slipping away.

"Sure and you don't think that you can actually surprise Fiona, do you? That woman knows everything," Aislinn grumbled.

Morgan threw up her hands, frustrated with everything today, and snagged her purse. "Fine, I'll go see Fiona. Happy?"

"Sure and she'll love the help," Aislinn sang after her and Morgan rolled her eyes as she stepped into the courtyard. Her rusty old van was parked by the fence. The door groaned when she opened it, stepping up to situate herself on the cracked leather seat. A rosary hung around the rearview mirror though why Morgan kept it there after what the nuns had done to her was beyond her. She supposed there was a small part of her that still believed in some sort of otherworldly presence…be it the Catholic God or not. Some nights, when things had been really tough, she would take the rosary down and run the smooth wood beads between her fingers while she tried to sleep in the back of the van and pretend like everything was going to work out just fine.

She supposed it had worked out so far.

Something in the engine squealed its protest as Morgan started the van and she waited a few minutes until the motor chugged to life. She knew that she would probably look at more reliable transportation, but this van had been the first home she could call her own and Morgan was reluctant to part with it.

The day played through her mind as her van lumbered down the road leading out of the village and along the cliffs that jutted so proudly from the sea. Aislinn was right, it was a beautiful day for a drive. The warm light from the sun kissed the jagged edges of the cliffs and the sea gleamed a bright turquoise that begged for people to swim in it.

Morgan had learned long ago not to be fooled by the whimsy of the water. It was still too early in the season for a true swim, though she loved watching tourists squeal in shock when they jumped in this time of year.

She nibbled at her bottom lip as the events of the day caught up with her. After a session with Baird, she always felt a little emotionally depleted, as though a wound that was healing kept reopening. Though Morgan knew it was part of the process, it often left her on edge for the rest of the day. The situation with Patrick had just topped off the emotional upheaval that she could handle for the day.

So what was she doing driving out to see Fiona? Morgan shook her head at herself. Maybe she was just a glutton for punishment.

Or maybe she just had nowhere else to turn.

A weathered sign tucked in a low stone wall indicated the turn for Fiona's lane and Morgan took it, bumping slowly up a gravel road as she approached a pretty gray cottage. Cheerful flowers were tucked in window boxes even though it was a bit early in the spring for them. It spoke of home and welcoming.

Her eyes trained on the cottage, Morgan turned off the engine, and pulled the key from the ignition, tucking it in her sun visor. She stared at the front door as she got out of the van and stood there, not knowing what to do. On a sigh, Morgan turned and for the first time, she saw the view.

It was like a punch to the gut. So raw, so stunning, that Morgan could understand the need for isolation. And yet, she'd never be lonely here. There was so much to see. Acres of green meadows rolled away from the cottage before falling off the edge of steep cliffs that thrust arrogantly into the sky. It was as though she stood at the edge of the world, and anything and everything was possible.

Mist clouded her eyes and Morgan pinched herself, surprised to find that tears were welling up. A bark startled her and she turned as sixty pounds of fur and slobber bounded around the corner and skidded to a halt in front of her feet.

"Oh, aren't you just a darling?" Morgan choked out, swiping the backs of her hands against her eyes. Helpless not to, she crouched and wrapped her arms around the dog. When he stayed still and turned to lick her face, something cracked inside Morgan.

Tears poured from her as she pressed her face into his soft fur, hugging the dog as though her life depended on it. Morgan didn't know what she was crying for. It was as though everything had come to a head in her life, both good and bad, and she had no idea how to handle people's expectations of her. Or even her own expectations of her. A part of Morgan was tempted to hop in her van and move on, living the life of a transient, never having to form bonds or deal with messy emotional entanglements.

"Thanks, buddy," Morgan whispered to the dog as he continued to swipe his rough tongue across her cheeks, cleaning her tears.

"Ronan's a good shoulder to cry on."

Morgan's shoulders tensed at the voice and straightening she turned to see Fiona leaning against the cottage. The old woman wore an oversized men's button-down shirt, work pants, and had a straw hat on her head with a cheerful flower tucked in the brim.

"Perhaps I should get a dog then," Morgan said stiffly and stroked Ronan's soft ears.

"Perhaps you should," Fiona agreed, "though that would require you to form an attachment, you know."

Morgan rolled her eyes at Fiona and sighed.

"Sorry to bother you, Fiona; Aislinn suggested that you might need help with some tonics so I drove out here."

"Is that why? Hmm," Fiona said, her warm eyes crinkling at the corners with a smile.

Morgan shrugged, feeling helplessly uncomfortable and not sure how to proceed.

"Well, come along then, I've got some bread just out of the oven for you and a nice stew."

So, Aislinn was right. The old woman did know everything.

"Can Ronan come inside?"

Fiona laughed and opened the door; Ronan raced inside and did several circles in the corner before he settled onto a pile of blankets with a bone.

"He's been a lovely companion for me," Fiona murmured as she stepped inside, motioning for Morgan to follow.

The cottage was essentially one large room, with two doors off of it leading to what Morgan presumed were bedrooms. It was larger inside than she had originally taken it for. The piece de resistance was a long wood farm table that dominated the middle of the room; it seemed to beckon to her to come sit. Long shelves lined the walls behind it and were cluttered with every size bottle imaginable, all labeled in a delicate script. Tall windows lined the wall to her left, leaving an uninterrupted view of the sea. To her right, a little alcove jutted off where a wood-burning stove and a few chairs were tucked. A few books were stacked next to the chair and Morgan imagined it made for a cozy reading nook.

"Tea? Whiskey?" Fiona asked, turning from the counter where she was slicing a loaf of brown bread. Steam rose from the bread and Morgan's mouth watered. There was nothing quite like a fresh loaf of Irish brown bread, she thought.

"Tea, please, though the whiskey is tempting," Morgan admitted.

"Tea it is, then. Go ahead, have a seat," Fiona instructed and Morgan moved to the long table and sat, looking at the pile of herbs and twine that covered the table.

"What are you making?"

"Ah, just drying some herbs for some creams. I've yet to get started on my tonics. Most likely I'll be doing those by moonlight."

"Why?" Morgan asked, looking up at Fiona.

"A touch of magick, of course," Fiona said with a smile and placed an earthenware bowl of stew in front of Morgan along with a napkin-lined basket of brown bread. She followed it up with a crock of butter and a sparkling glass of iced tea. Morgan was in heaven.

"Go on, eat. I don't have enough people enjoying my cooking these days," Fiona ordered and Morgan did as she was told, grateful for a reprieve in the conversation. She wasn't going to touch Fiona's comment about magick with a ten-foot pole, she thought. Fiona chuckled from across the room and Morgan raised an eyebrow at her.

The old woman moved with a grace that belied her years as she poured herself a dash of Irish and then brought her own bowl of stew to the table. Easing herself into her seat, she eyed Morgan across the table.

"Rough day?"

Morgan was surprised to find that she could smile at that. Perhaps her cry on Ronan had done some good for her after all.

"Rough life, more like it," Morgan muttered.

"Not as much anymore though; it seems like things are on the up and up for you," Fiona observed.

Morgan shrugged her shoulder and nodded, unsure of how much she wanted to say or what she wanted to reveal.

"Morgan, I owe you an apology," Fiona said.

The piece of bread that Morgan was holding dropped from her fingers into her soup and she stared at Fiona in confusion.

"Whatever for?"

"I...well, I do my best to find others like us across Ireland. Somehow you slipped past me. If I had known, I would have come for you. I would have taken you in, taught you about your powers. It's my fault that you went through what you did," Fiona said, her lips pressed into a tight line, her heart in her eyes.

"Oh...oh God," Morgan breathed, pressing the backs of her hands to her eyes as tears filled them again. "It's not your fault, Fiona. It's not anyone's fault really. Sometimes things just happen."

But if felt good. Knowing that someone would have taken her in. Maybe that would be enough for her, Morgan thought as warmth spread through her.

"It's not my fault that you were abused by those awful nuns, or that you bounced from home to home, but it most certainly is my fault for not finding you. I pride myself at being more knowledgeable than that. It must be because I heard nothing of your mother. Not a word. I still know nothing. Do you know anything?" Fiona asked carefully, her eyes trained on Morgan's.

Morgan sat back and wiped her eyes again, forcing her breath to calm.

"I don't. Not really. Mary McKenzie was her name, so I've kept that last name. They don't even know if she died or not to be honest. I was…I was found wrapped in blankets in a cardboard box on the steps of the Friary. She…she didn't even put me in a basket or anything." Morgan's voice stuttered a bit and she took a deep breath and continued. "A note was pinned to me that had my name on it and that she was giving up all rights to me. She signed it and everything. They never found her or any of my family. I don't even know if McKenzie is my real name."

"That may be it," Fiona said, pointing a finger at Morgan. "In fact…I wonder…" Her voice trailed off as she studied Morgan.

Feeling raw, and not caring, Morgan dipped into Fiona's mind to see what she was wondering. She jerked when she realized she was blocked. Heat crept up her cheeks in embarrassment.

"Yes, I learned to shield myself a long time ago, dear," Fiona said, dismissing Morgan's attempt to read her mind. She looked lost in thought for a moment and then seeming to come to a decision, she smiled at her.

"Knowing what I do now, I suspect that I may know or be able to find your mother…or at least what happened to her," Fiona said gently.

Time slowed for a second and Morgan could feel her heart beating in her chest as Fiona's words washed through her.

"I could find your mother."

Chapter Eleven

THE THOUGHT OF finding her mother was so incomprehensible to Morgan that she didn't even know what to say. It simply had never occurred to her to try and do so. She'd operated on the assumption that her mother was dead or long gone. It wasn't like she'd ever tried to check on her or see if she needed anything.

"I think that ship has sailed," Morgan said softly.

"Why do you say that?"

"Because if she was alive and had wanted to find me, well, she could have. It's obvious that she wanted nothing to do with me, so why bother hunting her down?" Anger and accusation laced her words and Morgan struggled to tamp down the deeply buried anger that she held.

"Maybe, maybe not. Perhaps something prevented her from finding you. Or maybe she knew that you were better off without her."

"Better off? Being shuttled from home to home? Being abused by the nuns? Running away at sixteen because it was so awful? How in the hell is that better?" Morgan shoved back from the table, standing to pace as she raged at Fiona. "Don't speak of what you don't understand, old woman."

Fiona rose herself and the kindness in her eyes almost broke Morgan.

"I know what it is to be a mother. Something of which you have no idea. And I know that sometimes you have to make choices in the best interests of your child. She might have thought that she was doing the best by you."

"She knew! She *knew* that I would have a power. She knew that they would consider me a freak. She knew it and she left me. She just left me…" Morgan's voice trailed off as tears overtook her and the walls of the cabin closed in around her. Turning, she pushed towards the door and stumbled outside, blinded by her rage. Rounding the corner of the cottage, she stumbled to her knees before curling in a ball, her back against the warm stones of the cottage, as she buried her face in her knees.

Finding her mother? How could Aislinn have sent her here to open this wound? Her anger reached out and encompassed Aislinn, Baird…the whole town. It had been stupid of her to come here. Stupid of her to dig all of this up. She'd learned long ago that to be a survivor meant putting her walls up and never showing her emotions.

She jumped as a tongue lapped her arm. Peeking out of her arms, she saw Ronan, his tail wagging, his nose inches from her face. He nuzzled into her, forcing her to raise her arm so he could push his nose into her face and lick her tears. Beside herself, and feeling emotionally raw, Morgan sighed and wrapped her arms around Ronan.

A movement to her left caught her eye and Fiona eased herself down onto the grass next to her, leaning against the wall.

"I'm sorry, Morgan. I can't speak for your mother or make assumptions on her behalf," Fiona said quietly.

"I…I'm sorry for yelling at you."

"It's okay. I suspect that you have a few years' worth of anger in there to get out. I'll just say it straight out…you were treated unfairly. But, just because you were dealt a raw deal doesn't mean you need to move forward in anger. Forever untrusting of others, never forming bonds. I want to help you. In fact, I promise to help you. No matter how many times you yell at me, no matter how mean you are to me, you won't be able to push me away. That's a promise that I make to you, here and now. Someone needs to stand for you. I wasn't able to before, but I'll be that person for you now."

Fiona's words flowed over her, soothing her soul, tamping down the fiery rage that filled her gut. Morgan brought her hands to her face as she all out sobbed, the tears falling down her cheeks and coursing beneath her palms to drip onto her pants.

She'd never had anyone to stand for her before.

"I need help," Morgan said, pulling her hands away and turning to look into Fiona's kind eyes. "I need all sorts of help. With my emotions, with learning to manage my powers. I can't even kiss a guy without my powers going haywire!"

Fiona laughed a little and then reached out, tentatively at first, to wrap her arm around Morgan's shoulders. Hesitant, but enjoying the comfort she provided, Morgan allowed herself to lean into Fiona.

"Patrick?"

"Aye, Patrick," Morgan whispered, staring out at the sea.

"Tell me what happens when you kiss."

"I…I just lose myself. It feels so amazing. But, that loss of control means everything goes to hell with my power."

Morgan detailed how the pint when flying and why she was scared to move forward with Patrick.

"And this has only happened while you were kissing him?"

"Well, it also happens when I sleep. Um, during my nightmares specifically."

"You have nightmares?" Fiona drew away so she could meet Morgan's eyes, concern etched on her face.

Morgan nodded and continued to rub Ronan's ears, happy for the comfort that the dog provided. Maybe she really did need to get a dog, she thought.

"The same one. It's all very gothic and dark, much more vivid and scary than the experience was in real life. There is chanting in Latin, candlelight flickering, my wrists are bound, and crosses are held over me. All very 18th century exorcism style, I guess."

"Yet this happened to you in real life."

Morgan nodded. "It did, but not nearly as gothic and dark as that. Pretty much every few months or every time I got sent home from a foster home, the nuns would tie me to a bed and pray for me while Father dumped holy water on my head. At first I would yell, but eventually I would just lie there and close my eyes, determined to wait them out. They would eventually give up and go on their way."

"So, this darker experience...do you think it is your fears from that situation? Or, perhaps you are reliving an experience from one of our ancestors," Fiona mused.

Morgan whipped her head around to look at Fiona. The old woman had a considering look in her eye. Tucking her hair behind her ear, Morgan studied her.

"You think that I am channeling someone else's experience?"

"You might be. You know that some of our ancestors were persecuted as witches. An exorcism would have been right in line with what would be considered a first act of trying to cure them."

"I just, wow, I'd never even considered that."

"Yes, you may have been living through a modern-day witch hunt of sorts at the hand of the nuns," Fiona mused.

All of a sudden, it was as though the memory had no power over her anymore. Fiona had reframed it in a manner that allowed her to distance herself from it and instead of being ashamed of what had happened to her, Morgan could now group herself in with her ancestors.

"I never, *ever* considered that," Morgan breathed.

"Yes, well, it can be hard to see something objectively when you are so close to the situation," Fiona said.

"If I told you the dream do you think you could figure out who it was?" Morgan asked eagerly. The thought of chasing down an ancestor, an actual blood relative of hers, excited her.

"So you're okay with me finding your ancestors and yet you don't want to know about your mother?" Fiona observed.

"It seems absurd when you say it like that, doesn't it?" Morgan asked.

"Feelings aren't rational, my dear," Fiona said.

Morgan laughed when Ronan nosed her again, this time with a stick in his mouth.

"Fetch, is it?" She tugged the bedraggled stick from his mouth and tossed it into the air. The dog let out a joyous bark like all his Christmases had come at once and raced after the stick, a furry bullet slicing through the tall grass.

"No, it's not rational. But, I don't think that I am ready to know more about my mother. I guess that I'm learning to be okay with where I am at and building from there. Is that okay?" Morgan asked.

"Perfectly fine, dear. Now, let's go inside so I can pull out my book. I might be able to find your ancestors as well as figure out a few tricks we can work on with controlling your powers."

Chapter Twelve

IT MIGHT BE FROM your ancestors. Morgan shook her head again as she sipped on a small glass of whiskey in the reading cove of Fiona's cottage. A cheerful fire burned in the stove, warding off the hint of chill that still clung in the early spring evenings. Ronan curled at her feet, every once in a while letting out a sleepy snort, his feet moving with his puppy dreams.

It was perhaps the most comfortable and most welcoming place that Morgan had ever been in. If Fiona truly meant her words, then Morgan could start to consider this cottage like a second home.

She'd always been jealous of her schoolmates and how they'd so casually mentioned going home to their family, or talked about what posters they were putting up in their rooms. The best Morgan could ever do was briefly mention a place that she was staying at. And, most of those homes had strict rules. Posters of cute movie stars had never been taped to her walls. She'd grown so used to being on her own that being welcomed into a home by Fiona as part of her brood that she watched over was a surreal experience.

And a welcome one.

"Ah, okay, I think that I may have found something. Though, I need to dig a little deeper. Can you tell me more about your dream again…no so much what they were saying, but are there any identifying articles of clothing or jewelry?"

"Hmm, let me think about this for a moment. Usually I try not to remember these dreams at all," Morgan said.

"I don't blame you. But, if I could date this a bit, I might have a better idea whose experience you are reliving."

Morgan shuddered a bit, thinking about how someone else had gone through even worse treatment than she had.

"I remember dark robes, crosses of course, and a silver and gold cup of sorts."

Fiona peered at her over her worn leather book.

"Like a chalice?"

"Yes, I suppose that would be a good word for it. Yes, a chalice of sorts. It held the holy water with which they continue to draw crosses on my naked body."

"Were there any identifying marks on the chalice?"“

"Hmm, I guess it is hard to say. I know that it was silver with a gold band around it. There were probably marks but you'd have to be really close to it to see all of the design work."

"Does it look something like this?"

Fiona turned the book around and Morgan gasped at the hand drawing of an intricately designed chalice. The ink color was aged to a light brown and the paper that it was on looked like coffee had spilled across it.

"Yes, that's it."

"That's the Chalice of Ardagh, my dear. There is no known written history of its use. Only speculation. Didn't you learn about it in school?"

Shock wove its way through Morgan as she tried to connect one of Ireland's most famous treasures with the chalice that she had seen in her dream. She'd never bothered to connect the two images, but now that she had, certainty rang through her.

"It's the same chalice. Oh my God, do you think that I may have historical information on it use?"

"You may. You know there is speculation that there are two chalices, right? That the real Chalice of Ardagh is hidden in the cove."

Morgan's mouth dropped open and she turned in the smooth wood rocking chair, pulling her knees up and wrapping her arms around her legs until she was tucked in a little ball, waiting on Fiona's every word.

"I had not heard that. In fact, I know little of the cove other than it is for sure cursed, blessed, however you want to look at it."

Fiona cocked her head and studied Morgan. She took a small sip of her whiskey.

"What makes you say that?"

"Aside from Aislinn and Flynn telling me?"

"Yes." Fiona gestured with her whiskey glass for Morgan to continue.

Morgan shrugged her shoulders.

"I just feel it when we go in there on the boat. It's like passing through a thin veil or something. The curse, or magic, or whatever, seems to hold a weight. It presses against me a bit and part of me feels like if I held my hand to the air I could trail my fingers through it. I don't know how else to explain it," she said.

"You're the first of my girls to feel it," Fiona observed.

A warmth slipped through Morgan at Fiona's words. Her girls. She belonged somewhere. The thought almost made her giddy. Yet, a part of her wanted to reserve these emotions. She'd learned long ago that sometimes if it looked like it was too good to be true, it probably was. She would proceed with caution.

"I think that I have more than one particular ability," Morgan admitted.

"Yes, you're definitely the strongest of any of my girls too," Fiona hummed. "We'll get to that in a moment. Now, the chalice. Grace's Cove got its name from the

Great Grace O'Malley, our strong and powerful ancestor. She was credited with keeping much of Celtic heritage alive and was a phenomenal woman in her own right. When it was time for her to die, she made her way to the cove, along with her pregnant daughter. The night that she walked into the water, she and her daughter worked a very powerful magick. Adding to the spell was the birth of her granddaughter on the beach that very night."

Morgan gasped as she tried to imagine saying goodbye to a mother and welcoming a baby within the same moment. It was no wonder there was powerful magick at the cove.

"Those who know whispers of the story began to assume that much of Grace O'Malley's treasure followed her there. But, that isn't true. Only one thing did. The chalice. Now, what's interesting to me is that the same chalice was used on you in a dream. So, the question is, did it leave the cove at some point and was returned or was it used on Grace O'Malley during her lifetime? Because as far as I know, Grace was the one who did the pillaging; she was not the subject of any torture."

Morgan imagined that her eyes had grown to the size of saucers as she stared at Fiona so casually recounting the legend. It was hard to believe that these people existed in real life.

"Gosh, I really don't know. I am just learning about all of this," Morgan said and Fiona waved her words away.

"Of course, I don't expect you to know the answer to that. I wonder though…" Fiona tapped the arm of her rocking chair and studied the flames for a bit. She opened her mouth and then closed it, shaking her head a definitive no.

"What?"

"Ah, nothing. I was thinking we could try something to find out more information, but there is really no need to lead you through the trauma. All it would do is add to the story, it doesn't necessarily solve any of your current problems with nightmares. Though…hm," Fiona said again and pressed her lips into a tight line.

"Well, I can't really give you any feedback if you don't tell me what you are thinking about," Morgan said cautiously and Fiona laughed softly.

"You're right at that."

"So? Go on and tell me then. I'll let you know if I think it is worth it," Morgan said, gesturing to Fiona with her whiskey glass. The fire caught the warm honey tone of the liquid and Morgan admired it briefly before turning her eyes back onto Fiona.

"Well, two things occurred to me as an option. One is called regression therapy. Essentially, I would hypnotize you and lead you back through past lives. But, I'm not sure that would matter unless you were a soul reincarnated that was also a direct line of Grace O'Malley. The chances of that are slim."

Morgan felt her mouth hanging open again as Fiona bowled her over with her words.

"The other would just be a dream regression hypnosis. I'd walk you through the dream, get more details on it, and then figure out a way you can have power in the dream so it no longer hurts you."

"I don't know if it will hurt me anymore actually," Morgan said.

Fiona tilted her head and studied Morgan.

"Why?"

"I don't know, really. It is just something that you said…about my ancestors experiencing the same. It made me feel less alone and for some reason, the fear in that dream seemed to slip away."

"So it was the connection of knowing that you weren't alone that made it less scary for you."

"Aye, I suppose so," Morgan said, leaning down to scratch at Ronan's ears. "I think we should do the first option." Surprised at herself, she looked down at the glass of whiskey, wondering if the whiskey was causing her to make rash decisions.

"You do? Hmm," Fiona said and paged through her book. For a moment, silence except for the quiet crackle of the fire descended upon them.

"I don't know that I've heard much about Grace's daughter," Morgan said, breaking the silence.

"Margaret was her name, or sometimes called Maeve in the history books."

"Isn't your daughter named Margaret?" Morgan asked.

Fiona only smiled at her and resumed paging through the book.

"Why doesn't Maeve show up in the history books?" Morgan asked, deciding that she liked the name better than Margaret.

"We don't know. The last record we have of her is the night on the beach and that isn't even public record. She was frighteningly young when Grace died, probably only fifteen or so."

Morgan's stomach clenched a bit as she tried to imagine being pregnant, alone on a beach with no medical care, and having to watch your mother die as you went into labor.

"How did she get through that? She was so young," Morgan breathed, fighting back tears for Maeve's struggles.

"I don't know, Morgan. I really don't. I know that those were different times. People were stronger then. There were more expectations placed upon them, and surviving was a daily battle. I suspect that Maeve had already built up a fairly tough exterior by that point. But, my heart still grieves for her."

Something flashed through Morgan, a sense of understanding, a knowing.

"I want to do the regression."

"If you are sure?"

"Right now, tonight."

Fiona drew back and looked at her, laying the old book in her lap.

"Why tonight?"

"It seems as though I am on a path of enlightenment today. Why stop now?" Morgan shrugged, unable to put into words her feeling of absolute certainty that she needed to do this regression tonight.

"I don't know if it is wise, Morgan. I feel that since you already feel better about your nightmares, it might be best to leave well enough alone."

"What's the worst that could happen?" Morgan asked, realizing that she sounded like a line in a B horror movie, right before the hapless lead character enters the woods.

"You might find out something that could change you forever."

Chapter Thirteen

THAT MIGHT BE A GOOD THING," Morgan found herself saying, surprised that she felt that way. "Maybe, I need this to feel complete."

Fiona studied her a moment before rising, Ronan at her heels, to cross the room to the door. She pushed the latch down and locked the door. Morgan's eyes tracked her as she went around the room, pulling the shutters closed on all of the windows. Fiona turned and motioned to Morgan.

"Let's do this in the guest room. You'll be more comfortable if you can lie down."

Her throat dry, Morgan swallowed and stood, a strange humming running down her skin. She felt overly sensitized, like she was about to step into another world.

"Morgan, I want to caution you again about this. You might not feel complete at all after this. Past life regressions often open up more questions than they do answers."

Morgan shrugged, affecting a calmness that she certainly didn't feel.

"It will be fine. It won't be the worst thing that I have gone through in my life."

Fiona stopped and turned to look at her again, her hand on the door to the bedroom.

"You don't know that."

A shiver trickled down Morgan's spine and she straightened, surprised to find that Fiona's words made her angry.

"And you don't know that this might be the best thing for me. So don't go all doom and gloom on me, okay?" Miffed, Morgan shot her chin into the air and sailed past Fiona into the bedroom.

A warm chuckle followed her.

"That's the spirit," Fiona commented and then went across the room to a small chest of drawers. "Go on, make yourself comfortable," she called over her shoulder, digging around in the drawers.

Morgan turned towards the single bed tucked under an alcove with a window that overlooked the water. Whitewashed walls and a hand-stitched quilt completed the simple corner, and in its own way, it was soothing. No distractions, this room seemed to say. Just be.

Moving to the edge of the bed, she sat, running her fingers over the intricate design in the quilt. Morgan could all but feel the love pulsing from the soft fabric. This was a safe spot, she could feel it down to her core.

"What do you know of reincarnation?" Fiona asked, coming to the bed and laying a variety of items on the bedside table. She turned and pulled a chair from a corner.

What did she know of it? Morgan shrugged. "Not much, I guess. I know that the nuns believe that we go to heaven. And I know that we come back in other lifetimes. I guess that I don't know how I know that, I just do?" Her voice went up a note at the end of her words, uncertain, yet certain at the same time.

"We do come back. But, from what I gather, we come back to learn more. Each time around, we are working something out. Our souls have a lesson to learn while we are here."

Morgan nodded, watching as Fiona began to place crystals around the bed.

"So what do you think that I am here to learn?"

Fiona turned and met her eyes.

"What do you think you are here to learn about?"

"I…I don't know. I guess I've never really thought about it. Abandonment, maybe. Or just feeling like I matter, I guess." Morgan shrugged off the words, not yet ready to deal with the emotions behind them.

"Well, I can tell you that you are worth something. But, until you feel it, my words won't matter much," Fiona observed. She sat and clasped Morgan's hands, searching her face with her brandy-colored eyes.

"Will this help me?" Morgan whispered.

"It might. But knowing is only the first step. You've a ways to go before you heal yourself. Let's see what happens." Fiona gestured for Morgan to lie flat on the bed. Morgan leaned back, situating herself so her hair wasn't stuck under her. She stared up at the wood beams that crisscrossed the ceiling above her.

"So, how does this work?"

"I will lead you through a few relaxation exercises. I must tell you that you will always be in control. So, even if I lead you somewhere that you don't want to be, you have total power to leave that space. Understand me? You are in control. I am simply your guide."

Morgan was grateful for Fiona's explanation. Control was vitally important to her.

"Okay, thank you. I'm ready."

Morgan closed her eyes and waited, not sure what to expect.

"Morgan, I'd like you to begin by taking a few deep breaths, just allowing the muscles in your body to relax."

She drew a breath in, holding it for a moment, allowing it to reach all of her muscles, before exhaling in one slow breath. Repeating this, she began to soothe herself, doing her best not to try and attempt to read Fiona's mind to anticipate what would come next.

"Now, I'd like you to continue breathing like that, but imagine yourself at the top of a beautiful spiral staircase."

Morgan immediately pictured herself at the top of a wrought-iron spiral staircase. It just appeared beneath her, and there was nothing but a flat black floor around her. The only way to go was down.

"This staircase is leading down from where you are now, to even greater depths of your being, where greater levels of knowledge await you, where the truths you seek are waiting for you, the answers to every question. Know that as you descend this staircase, all that waits for you is truth, support, and healing. I will start counting slowly from the number 10 down to 1. When we reach 1, you will have arrived to the place where all the answers you are seeking may be found."

The pull of Fiona's voice was lulling Morgan into a soothing breathing pattern. She nodded slightly to show that she understood and as Fiona began to count, Morgan took the first step.

"Ten. You will begin the journey down. Start the journey down to the deepest, most knowing part of yourself.

"Nine. Deeper and deeper. You find yourself relaxing more."

Fiona's voice seemed to come from a great distance as Morgan descended the staircase in her mind, excited to see what lay at the bottom. Her hand trailed over the cool metal of the railing, and she circled the middle support, enjoying the spiraling of the staircase.

"Deeper still. Deeper and deeper. More and more relaxed. So peaceful. So deep. So peaceful. So deep. So beautiful. So deep."

Fiona's voice had taken on a hypnotic chant in the background, and Morgan allowed the words to carry her forward to the last step, knowing that she was cradled in the safety of Fiona's great powers.

She stopped at the bottom step and looked around her. The staircase ended in a dark room, and she couldn't see anything behind her. Turning her head towards the light source, Morgan gasped. It was like an entire wall of the room had been knocked out and the gentle sound of waves lapping on a beach reached to her. Light from the sun shot into the dark room, and Morgan held up her hand to shield her eyes, straining to see what lay beyond the walls of the room.

"You are now in a special and safe place. Know that you are protected as you step forward."

Fiona's words seemed to carry to her on a sea breeze that tickled her cheeks.

"Look down at yourself. Are you wearing anything?"

Surprised, Morgan looked down at herself. A gasp shot from her mouth and she covered her face with her hand, gaping down at herself.

"Is something wrong?"

"I'm pregnant! Hugely, hugely pregnant!" Morgan gasped out, completely in awe of the large belly that stuck out in front of her.

"Are you clothed?"

"Aye, I'm in a deep maroon gown of sorts. A woven cloth. It's seen better days, but for some reason, I feel like it is my best. I wear this with pride."

"A ceremonial robe?"

"Yes…yes. That feels right."

"What do you see around you?"

"I'm still standing at the bottom of the stairs. But, I can see what I think is a beach across the room from me. Should I go there?"

"Go ahead, you are safe to leave the staircase."

A thrill of excitement shot through Morgan as she left the staircase and began to walk towards the open wall. Instinctively, she rubbed her belly softly, making soothing circles across the great mound. Even her gait felt different, off-kilter from the weight of the child that lay within her womb.

The room seemed to fade behind her as she stepped into the sunlight, her bare toes pressing into the sand.

"It's the cove! I'm in the cove," Morgan exclaimed, holding her hand up to shield her eyes from the sun as she looked around at the rocky walls that hugged the cove. "It's the same. But different."

"How is it different?"

"There are just more rocks piled up on the walls…I don't know. I don't see a path up to the top either. I wonder how I got here."

"How do you feel being there?"

Morgan stopped and thought about it, staring out at the blue waters as they gently lapped against the sand beach. She should feel happy; her baby was to be born soon and it was a beautiful day.

"I feel incredibly sad. Oh, it hurts so much. I don't understand...why am I so sad?" Morgan gasped out, feeling tears well in her eyes.

"It's okay to feel sad. We all do at times. Are you alone there?"

"I...I don't know," Morgan said, wiping the back of her palm across her eyes as she turned to walk along the beach. A figure seemed to appear through a mist, her arms outstretched for Morgan. Without a thought, she found herself lumbering across the sand in a half-joyous, half-pained trot, desperately wanting to be with this person.

"Mother!" Morgan cried out, lost in the vision, no longer hearing Fiona's words.

Arms embraced her and Morgan could smell a faint scent of lavender and sea moss as she buried her face in the woman's shoulder, holding on as tight as her large belly would allow her.

"Who is your mother, Morgan?" Fiona's voice broke through the moment and Morgan looked up to see a stunningly beautiful woman looking down at her. This woman radiated strength as much as she did love.

"It's Grace. Grace is my mother," Morgan whispered.

"Which would make you Margaret O'Malley," Fiona whispered.

"Maeve," Morgan automatically corrected her, knowing it was right.

"Maeve it is then," Fiona murmured.

Morgan continued to hold her mother, needing the connection, knowing it wasn't long now. She didn't want her to go. She wasn't ready for this.

"No," Morgan said, whispering to the woman who stood before her.

"No, what?" Fiona asked.

"No, I don't want her to do it. I don't. She's going to walk into the water," Morgan gasped, tears running freely down her cheeks.

"Why is she doing this?" Fiona asked.

Morgan knew she was speaking with Grace, but the conversation seemed to flow past her. A thought flashed into her head.

"She has a blood disease. Something of the blood. She's dying. It's her time. I have to help her," Morgan gasped out.

"How are you helping her?"

"Magick," Morgan whispered, holding out her arm as Grace slashed a shallow slice across her left palm, and doing the same to hers. Placing her hand to Morgan's, she squeezed tight as she pulled Morgan into a circle of stones. Grace smiled at her with love and placed her free hand on Morgan's belly, completing the circle. Immediately, she began to chant.

"What's happening?" Fiona asked.

"She's cut my hand, blood is pouring down from us, her hands are on my belly now; she is blessing my child."

Morgan's face felt sticky and wet with tears as she stared down at the marks of blood across her belly, knowing the time was now. Grace leaned over, kissing her gently on the mouth, before she turned and raised her hands to the cove, crying the words that would forever enchant the waters with her power.

Morgan crossed her arms over her belly, falling to her knees as her mother, her life, walked slowly into the water, her arms raised above her head as she continued to chant.

"I don't want her to go. I'm so young. I'm so scared. I can't do this alone. I can't be a mother alone. How am I going to give birth without her?" Morgan's words panted out of her, real physical pain lashing through her as she thought about her mother leaving her. "Why is she abandoning me?"

"She is most likely saving you from having to care for her as the disease takes her body," Fiona suggested gently.

"If she's so powerful, why can't she save herself?" Morgan gasped, watching as the water crept up her mother's neck.

"Because we all must die. And then we come back. It was her time," Fiona said quietly.

"She's leaving me! The water…no, the water is going over her head…" Morgan cried out as the waves lapped over her mother's head and in an instant she was gone. "No, noooooo," Morgan said on a keening wail, sobbing as the most important person in her life disappeared into the sea. With a flash of light, the waters lit with a brilliant blue glow, so bright, so stunning, that Morgan had to shield her eyes from it.

"Shhh, Morgan, you're okay. You're safe," Fiona said.

"The cove is glowing," Morgan said quietly, her sobs coming more softly as a new and very real pain lashed through her lower back.

"What are you doing?"

"I'm…I think that I'm going into labor," Morgan said, her eyes wide with shock as she brought her hand to her back, standing slowly on the beach, staring into the waters, willing her mother to come back and help her.

"You can get through this, Morgan. Remember, we are all here because you birthed this child," Fiona reminded her.

"I don't know what to do. How can I do this without her? She left me!" Morgan screamed her anger and fear into the breeze that whipped around her, blowing her hair back from her face. The cove continued to pulse with a brilliant blue light.

"You can leave, you can come home," Fiona whispered.

"No, I have to do this," Morgan panted, walking the cove, staring at the water, silently blaming her mother for leaving her.

"I will coach you through it," Fiona said gently.

Morgan began to breathe, letting out little puffs of air as she walked the beach for hours, rubbing her back, crying as pain lashed through her.

"It's close. She's close," Morgan said, wondering how she knew that she was having a daughter.

"Why don't you kneel down," Fiona suggested.

"I have to go into the water," Morgan said, stumbling into the waves. The blue light surrounded her as she stood waist deep in the water and screamed, throwing her head back to the sky, crying out as she pushed her baby into the world. Bending over, she helped her daughter from her body, pulling her from the water that was lit from within.

"Oh God, I don't know what to do," Morgan panted, immediately putting her finger in her baby's mouth and clearing the gunk out.

"Clear her passages," Fiona instructed.

"I just did. I don't know why," Morgan said, looking blindly down at the infant she held in her arms.

On a small cough, the infant seemed to come to life with a hearty wail, the cries echoing off the walls of the cove. If it was possible, the cove seemed to glow even more intensely and for a moment, Morgan found herself laughing down at the squalling baby, relief and happiness coursing through her.

"I'll never leave you, little one. I'll always be with you," Morgan promised her, pulling her dress down to help her daughter begin to nurse. The joy of motherhood pierced her, cutting through her anger with Grace for leaving her, and in a small way, it began the path of healing her pain from losing Grace.

"Do you need to stay there anymore? Did you get what you needed?" Fiona asked.

Morgan turned and began to walk gingerly out of the water with her baby in her arms. Scanning the rock walls, she wondered how she would get out of here. Or even take care of her own body's physical needs.

But a part of her knew that it was time for her to go.

"It's time." Morgan nodded.

"Then I'd like you to turn back to the room that you came from, where the staircase is."

Morgan turned and saw the large cutout in the rock wall, the wrought-iron spiral staircase highlighted in the middle. Hesitantly, she stepped towards the staircase, crossing the sand with her baby in her arms.

"What will happen to my baby?" Morgan exclaimed, looking down at the infant in her arms.

"She's safe. I promise. Now go to the bottom of the stairs. Once there, you'll see that the infant is no longer in your arms."

Morgan stepped to the bottom of the staircase and looking down again, she was surprised to see that Fiona was right. Her baby was gone, as were the robes she had been wearing. Her normal clothes were back on her body. Whipping her head around, she looked out onto the beach and saw a brief glimmer of a maroon robe walking down the line of the sand.

"I'm going to count to ten. With each number, you'll go a little higher up the staircase. One." Fiona began and Morgan began to climb the staircase. With each step she pulled further away from the beach, leaving the anguish and loneliness behind her.

"Morgan," Fiona said gently at her side and Morgan blinked her eyes open, staring again at the rafters above her.

"I'm Maeve," Morgan gasped out, sitting up and clasping Fiona's hands. A dizziness washed through her and her head was swimming with crazy thoughts. Most notably, she felt a sense of excitement course through her. "I'm Maeve! I'm Grace's daughter! I know who I am...I belong here."

Fiona watched her cautiously and then reached out to stroke her hand down Morgan's cheek.

"No, you're Morgan McKenzie," Fiona said softly, concerned etched across her face.

Morgan laughed at her.

"No, I know that. But, I'm also Maeve. A part of me is Maeve!"

Fiona watched her carefully and then nodded.

"Come, let's get a drink. We need it."

Chapter Fourteen

"TELL ME EVERYTHING," Fiona instructed, as they sat once again in the rocking chairs, tucked in front of the fire, Ronan snoring again at their feet.

Morgan sipped her whiskey, recounting all the details of what she had just seen. Her head was spinning as she tried to remember every last moment, any tidbit that could be important to her.

"So now we know how the cove began its little light show trick," Fiona mused.

"I didn't know that it glowed," Morgan said.

"Aye, it does. In the presence of love," Fiona said and Morgan's heart warmed as she thought about the beautiful blue light that had surrounded her as she gave birth.

"It was a powerful experience," Morgan said softly, tracing her finger down the side of her glass.

"Yes, if you were to pick any moment in time to go back to, you sure picked a doozie," Fiona agreed.

"It felt good, you know, to see my mother, I guess any mother of mine," Morgan mumbled and buried her nose back into her glass.

Fiona raised an eyebrow at her. "Of course it would be. What do you think the lesson is there?"

Morgan shrugged, then forced herself to think about it.

"I suppose that I am here to learn how to make it on my own? To know that I am strong enough on my own?" Morgan asked, the words spilling from her mouth.

"Are you asking me or telling me?" Fiona asked.

"Both?" Morgan smiled weakly at her and Fiona smiled back.

"I think that your soul needs to learn that it is always loved, no matter whether your mother is there to see it or not," Fiona said gently.

"So, I just need to know that I am loved and that I am strong enough – good enough – to make it on my own," Morgan stated, taking another sip of her whiskey, letting the liquid warm its way down her throat.

"Easier said than done," Fiona commented and Morgan found herself smiling.

"You know…I think that I am getting there. This helped a lot. It gives me a piece of myself that I don't think I ever would have had. So, thank you for that," Morgan said.

"It helped me too. I now know even more about our history than I ever have before," Fiona mused.

"Though I don't think that I'd like to repeat that whole giving birth experience any time soon," Morgan said and Fiona chuckled.

"You really went through the trenches on that. I almost pulled you so you wouldn't have to experience it."

"I think that I needed to. To feel what I would do to protect that baby in my arms. To maybe get a glimmer of understanding on why Grace walked into the water. It was to protect me."

"Aye, yes. Grace was a powerful woman. If people had known she was sick, they would have challenged you, fought for your lands. Instead, she signed over her lands in the right manner and chose a private death with you there. It was a powerful decision made by a proud and powerful woman. I admire her," Fiona said.

"I suppose that I do as well," Morgan murmured, surprised to feel her eyelids beginning to droop.

"Ah, yes, you'll be feeling the effects of your experience. Why don't you go to bed? I'll get you a nice breakfast in the morning. Tomorrow's your day off?"

"I'm supposed to go with Flynn to the cove."

"I'll give him a call. He's right across the way and can come pick you up, if he still needs you to go."

Nodding, Morgan stood and turned, not sure if she should hug Fiona or thank her for her help. Fiona smiled gently up at her, patting her arm lightly.

“I know. Go on now, rest, my dear.”

Morgan was asleep before her head hit the pillow.

Chapter Fifteen

MORGAN BLINKED AWAKE, moving seamlessly from sleep to clarity. She stared at the rafters above the small bed and took a deep breath. She felt wonderful. It was the first time in a long time that she had slept peacefully, no dreams to shock her awake. Stretching, Morgan rolled to her side when she felt a cold nose press into her arm.

"And a good morning to you, Sir Ronan," Morgan whispered over the edge of the bed, running her hand over his silky ears and smiling when he lapped his tongue across her palm. Morgan swung her feet over the side of the bed and stood, crossing the room to make use of the small bathroom attached to her room.

As she washed her hands, Morgan studied her face in the small wooden mirror tucked above the pedestal sink. For the first time in ages, her moody blue eyes seemed to shine, and the skin beneath them wasn't puffy or marred with dark circles.

The past-life regression had been a tremendous gift, she thought. Though it had been terribly overwhelming, and incredibly sad, it has also gifted Morgan with a sense of her background – of where she came from – that she had never known before. And, a part of her was secretly proud of herself for having given birth alone and somehow managing to get out of the cove alive. She wondered what had happened to Maeve after that and made a note to work with Fiona about researching more of Maeve's story.

Morgan splashed cold water on her face and patted it dry with a soft cotton towel that hung near the sink. Feeling lighter, if not almost a bit wiser, Morgan wandered into the main room to see what Fiona was about.

"Ah, you've risen. How did you sleep?" Fiona put down a bowl that she was mixing at the counter and crossed to Morgan, clasping Morgan's face between her weathered hands and searching Morgan's eyes.

Morgan smiled and bent down to press a kiss to her papery cheek.

"Better than I have in years, actually."

"Really? How fascinating," Fiona murmured and turned to walk back to her bowl. Today the old woman wore a long woven skirt and a loose cotton blouse. She must not be planning to go into the fields, Morgan thought.

"Really. I don't know. I feel good. Like I know myself a little better. I don't know, it's like my confidence has grown a bit," Morgan said, pulling out a chair at the table and sitting down to prop her head up in her hands.

"Because you know who you are?" Fiona asked.

"Maybe. Or maybe it is because I went through the experience of giving birth and know that I survived. Or, perhaps it is simply getting true validation that our souls do come around again. It's comforting, you know? Kind of makes everything not seem so serious." Morgan shrugged, wishing that she could put her feelings into words better.

"Sure and I can understand that. There is great comfort in knowing that this isn't it for us. It's why people have sought out religion for thousands of years. We all seek to gain the knowledge that we are going to be okay."

"Yes, that's true. I…I think it will help me to not take myself so seriously," Morgan said.

Fiona turned and raised an eyebrow at her.

"You mean with Patrick?"

Heat crept up Morgan's cheeks and she nodded. Tucking her hair behind her ear, she thought about it a bit more. "With Patrick, or with anything. I obsess over what people will think of me, if they will like me, if I'll be accepted. It's one of the reasons that I stay away from forming relationships. I'm worried that people won't like me or that I'll let them down. I think that I'll be able to ease some of that anxiety now. Maybe." Morgan shrugged again and smiled up at Fiona as she brought her a pot of breakfast tea.

"That's a very astute observation," Fiona said.

"Ah, well, Baird's been helping me, I guess."

"He's a good man," Fiona observed.

"He is. I do feel comfortable with him and I love him and Aislinn together."

"Yes, they make a good team. He's steadfast and logical which makes a good contrast to Aislinn's dreamy, creative side."

"Yes, they balance each other well." Morgan blew on her tea before pouring cream into the cup, watching the swirl of light and dark liquids mix together.

"And how do you think Patrick will balance you?"

Morgan felt a sliver or excitement go through her before panic set in. She gripped the mug and stared down at its contents, unsure of what she thought.

"I don't know. I've never been in a relationship before. I don't know how to," Morgan admitted.

"Why don't you start by making him dinner?" Fiona suggested as she slid a plate with a Full Irish in front of Morgan. Morgan stared down at all of the food in dismay and then looked up at Fiona, her heart in her eyes.

"I...I don't know how to cook."

Fiona stopped and stared at her, her mouth open in surprise. She clenched her hands into fists and placed them on her hips.

"Now that is positively un-Irish. Alright then, I see we have a lot of work to do. Can you stay here today? I'll teach you a meal and one trick for controlling your powers when Patrick kisses you. It will at least start you in the right direction."

Warmth spread through Morgan and she smiled up at Fiona, grateful for her, happy that Aislinn had pushed her into coming out here. It had been the right step for her and Morgan wondered why she had fought it for so many months.

"I'm assuming Flynn doesn't need me today as it's already mid-morning?"

Fiona lifted a hand and waved it in the air.

"I told him that I was stealing you for today. He was fine with it."

For a moment, Morgan felt angry that Fiona had made this decision for her. Then she remembered that she wasn't supposed to take things so seriously, and she let the anger go. Flynn would understand. She'd still be able to work with him next week. It would all be okay. Blowing out a small breath, she smiled at Fiona before digging in to her eggs before they got cold.

"So what do you eat then?" Fiona asked. "You've a lovely figure, but I wonder if you are getting enough nutrition."

Morgan rolled her eyes and laughed, but it felt good, knowing that someone cared about her health.

"I eat fairly simply. Apples, carrots, those kinds of grab-and-go healthy foods. Sandwiches with some meat. That type of stuff. I don't eat a lot so my grocery bill isn't much." Morgan shrugged.

"Do you know how to cook meat?" Fiona asked, her head cocked.

"Not really. In a pan?" Morgan asked and Fiona sighed.

"Okay, let's start simple. Men are fairly easy to please so I am thinking spaghetti and meatballs along with some garlic bread should do the trick. What is your kitchen like? Do you have a stove?"

"I do, though it is tiny. I was surprised though. I just expected a cook top or something of that nature, but I have an oven. Shane outfits his properties well," Morgan said.

"Aye, perfect. Okay, we'll start your lessons when you are finished."

Morgan looked down at her plate, surprised to see that she had eaten her way through two-thirds of the food. Pushing it away, she stood and took the plate to the sink.

"I'm finished. Usually I just have a banana for breakfast." Morgan shrugged and rinsed her plate in the sink, her eyes drawn to the view of the cove. "Sure and this is a lovely spot to cook at. Just look at that view."

Fiona joined her at the sink and looked out of the window with her.

"It is. I once tried to live away from here, and it just never felt right. After my husband passed, it made no sense to try and live in the city anymore. This spot is home. It makes my heart happy and that is all that matters to me."

"Do you miss him?" Morgan asked, turning to look down at Fiona.

"Aye, at times, I miss him so badly that I want to curl up in a ball and die. I don't know if that ever goes away. But, it's been over thirty years since he's been gone. You learn to live with it, even if you don't want to."

"What was he like?"

"Oh, John was just…larger than life. His laughter, his heart, he did everything big. Our house was always full with friends; he was legendary for his stories. I miss him," Fiona said simply and turned to put the dishes on the drying rack. "Alright, enough reminiscing. Which do you want to start with? Cooking or learning to control your powers?"

Morgan straightened, her palms feeling a little sweaty, as she tried to decide which would be the lesser of two evils.

"Powers." She decided.

Fiona nodded and motioned for Morgan to follow her. They reached the door leading outside and Fiona snagged a worn leather book, the same she had been reading the night before, from the table before opening the door and allowing Ronan to dart out into the sunshine. Together, they stepped outside and Morgan followed Fiona around the cottage to where a small table and chairs were set next to the cottage. Morgan smiled as Ronan raced across the fields and then gasped as another dog shot across the ridge behind them and down into the field to meet up with Ronan.

"That's Teagan, Flynn and Keelin's dog. She and Ronan are best friends."

Morgan watched them circle each other and then race across the fields together, their ears streaming back in the wind. It pinched at her heart, just a bit. She wanted to have that freedom and ease with someone in her life.

They settled onto the chairs and Morgan closed her eyes for a bit, reaching out with her power in her mind to allow the energy of nature to pulse at her. If someone had asked what she was doing, she wouldn't have been able to explain it. At best, it was almost like feeling the energy of the natural world. She did this sometimes, usually when she was angry or upset, and it soothed her. There was something so raw and beautiful about nature and the energy that it emitted that it would inevitably calm her down and show her how petty her anger was.

"What are you doing?" Fiona asked.

Morgan opened her eyes and smiled at Fiona and shrugged. "Just, uh, feeling the energy here, I guess."

"Like Aislinn then? You know that is part of how she paints, right?"

"Yes, I suppose that it is the same. Though I'm not creative like she is." Morgan shrugged.

"I find it fascinating that you have a touch of what each of my girls have. Except, I haven't asked you about the healing. Can you heal?"

"I honestly don't know. I've never tried."

"Do you ever get scrapes or bruises and massage them with your hand? They disappear right after?"

Morgan thought about it. She was often scraping herself throughout the day on Flynn's fishing boats. It was normal for those in an active lifestyle and she didn't know many fishermen that weren't used to nicks and scrapes as part of their daily routine. She looked down at her arms, and saw no marks there.

"I suppose that I do, though I've never though about it. In fact, I have no scars anywhere," Morgan said, looking down at herself and lifting her arms to look.

Her heart stopped.

Just for a second, panic raced through her. *Breathe, Morgan, just breathe*, she told herself.

"What happened? What's wrong?" Fiona said, standing over her, running her hands over Morgan's body, feeling for something.

Morgan held up her left hand, palm up. A thin white ridge sliced across her palm, a scar that looked like it had been there forever.

Except it hadn't.

Fiona reached for her hand, running her finger over the smooth white line that broke the creases in her palm.

"This wasn't there yesterday, was it?"

Morgan shook her head, unable to comprehend how living through a remembered past in her soul could bring to surface the scar.

"This is powerful magick," Fiona whispered and leaned down to press a kiss to Morgan's palm. "This is also an incredible gift. I think she wanted you to remember that you aren't alone. Whenever you doubt yourself or feel lonely, look down at that scar and know that you are loved."

Morgan swallowed past the lump that had formed in her throat, unable to comprehend or process all of the emotions that were swarming through her. She closed her palm and brought it to her lap, running her fingers over the smooth ridge in her palm. As a reminder, it was a brilliant one.

"How could this happen? I don't understand," Morgan said.

"I don't quite know. Yet, the power of Grace O'Malley never ceases to surprise me."

Turning, Fiona gestured to the objects she had placed on the table. A few rocks, a crystal, a stick, and a cup.

"First, I'd like to see how your power works. You're the first that I know of that can move inanimate objects. Can you do that for me?"

Morgan raised an eyebrow at her and then, reaching out with her mind, she visualized the cup rising into the air. The cup did as she asked, hovering two feet above the table, staying completely still in the air.

"Wow, just wow," Fiona murmured. "It doesn't even shake."

"I can hold it like this while I talk," Morgan said, not looking at the cup; instead her eyes followed the dogs across the fields.

"So you don't even have to watch it?"

"Nope." Morgan shrugged.

"Can you hold more than one thing at a time?"

Morgan smiled, and for the first time really enjoying showing off her power, she lifted every item on the table and circled them around Fiona.

Fiona's warm brandy eyes lit with delight as she watched the items dance around her. They swooped in a circle and then lined up in front of them both, hovering about four feet off of the grass.

Like a bullet, Ronan shot across the lawn and launched himself into the air, snagging the stick neatly from the line of objects in the air and landing adeptly, before racing across the grass again.

"Ronan!" Morgan shouted out a peal of laughter, as did Fiona, the objects dropping to the grass in front of them.

"I guess we shouldn't use a stick for this. That's my fault," Fiona laughed, wiping tears from her eyes.

"Though I could really add to his game of fetch." Morgan laughed and laughed, having fun with her powers for the first time in her life.

"Oh, he would just love that. Maybe when we are finished here you can play with him a bit."

"Yes, I will." Morgan smiled at Fiona.

"So, I noticed that when you were startled, the items dropped from the air. Why did that happen?"

Morgan thought about it. "I stopped visualizing them in the air, I guess."

"And yet, when you are distracted, like during a kiss, objects will levitate."

"Yes."

"So there is a correlation somewhere with focusing and not focusing. I'm not sure quite what it is yet, because it almost seems like the relationship is inverted, but I have been thinking about a way that you can visualize turning off your power during particular moments."

"I'm all ears," Morgan said, waving at Fiona to continue. She stretched her legs out in front of her, leaning back against the table. The breeze tickled her face and carried the scent of sea with it.

"I think you should visualize it like an electrical current. You turn it on or off. So, for example, if Patrick leans in for a kiss, visualize a big switch in your head where you flip the power off. You'll need to practice this a bit, but I think the stronger you become at it, the more you'll be able to control the latent use of your ability."

Morgan pursed her lips, considering Fiona's words carefully. The image of a huge switch, the kind that had a handle that you pulled down to shut off the lights in a warehouse, formed in her mind.

"So, first, visualize the switch."

Morgan nodded and flicked a finger in the air, gesturing for her to go on.

"Now that you have the switch, imagine all of these currents of energy running through you that connect to the switch. Right now it is in the on position. I'd like you to turn it off."

Morgan leaned back and closed her eyes, feeling like a thousand volts of energy ran through her to the switch in her head. In her mind, she grabbed the switch and slammed it down, turning it off.

"Now raise that cup off the grass."

Morgan focused on the cup on the grass. Reaching out, she tried to raise it from the ground. It sat there, looking out of place in the grass, never moving an inch.

"I'll be damned, it worked," Morgan said in awe, turning to Fiona. "It really worked. I've never not been able to move something before."

Fiona smiled and patted her arm, instructing her to flip the switch back on.

Morgan imagined the switch again and in her mind, she flipped the switch to the on position. A current of energy pulsed through her and in seconds, the cup was hovering in front of their faces.

"Seems as though you're a quick learner," Fiona observed.

Morgan stared at the cup, her mouth hanging open, before happiness rushed through her. On a squeal, she wrapped her arms around Fiona, hugging the old woman with all her might.

"It worked! I can control it!" Morgan exclaimed, feeling happier than she had in years.

"So it seems that it is time to move on to the harder lesson then." Fiona sniffed and rose. "Let's test your mettle in the kitchen."

Morgan groaned and rose, knowing that cooking would truly be her hardest lesson of the day. Following Fiona, she did a little skip in the grass.

Finally, she was in control.

Chapter Sixteen

LATER THAT DAY, MORGAN climbed the steps to her apartment, armed with her new knowledge. She needed a shower, and she needed to get to the market. But first, she wanted to scan through her wardrobe to see if she had anything pretty to wear.

Her nerves hummed with energy as she flipped between her shirts, finally settling on a deep red V-neck top that complemented her skin and brought out her eyes. Snagging her skinny jeans, she tossed the clothes on the bed, and jumped in the shower, pushing the thought of what she was about to embark on out of her mind.

He probably had to work all night, Morgan thought as she scrubbed her body with a citrus scrub that Fiona had sent home with her. She inhaled the orangey scent, loving the way it seemed to wake her up and excite her senses.

Making a mental note to tell Fiona that she'd like to package a few bottles and sell it at the cash register in the gallery, Morgan stepped from the shower and toweled off.

Eyeing herself in the mirror, she decided that tonight called for makeup. Morgan bent and pulled a brightly patterned makeup bag from beneath the sink. Leaning forward, she squinted as she tried to apply eyeliner.

"Damn it," Morgan cursed as she drew a sloppy line across her eye. Blowing out a breath, she grabbed a tissue and wiped it off. No eyeliner then.

Instead, she began to shadow her eyes, deepening the crease above them, and making their slant more exaggerated. They almost looked like cat eyes, she decided. Brushing the tips of her eyelashes with a coat of mascara, she finished up with a slick of lip gloss. Tilting her head in the mirror, she eyed her long mane of hair. Rarely did Morgan do anything with her hair as it hung so straight. Thinking about it, she pulled some strands from the temple area and created a braid on both sides, pulling them both back and securing them at the back of her head. It almost looked a bit like a crown, she thought as she tucked a loose strand in. A hippie, wildflower type crown maybe. Shaking her head at herself, she went to her dresser drawer, eyeing her underwear choices. Morgan sighed.

"Could you be any more uninteresting?" she wondered out loud as she looked down at her drawer of white cotton underwear and white bras. Pulling out the set with the lace edging, she made another mental note to go shopping with her next paycheck. It was time to grow up.

Morgan tried to imagine herself as some daring woman of the world, wearing all black, and brilliantly colored sexy underwear, leaving a trail of broken hearts and heavy perfume in her wake. She laughed.

"That is so not going to happen."

She finished getting dressed, deliberately ignoring her nerves and every part of her that wanted to curl up on the couch with a book and not leave her apartment. Looking down at the scar on her hand, Morgan reminded herself that it was important to take chances.

"Here we go," she said as she grabbed her shopping tote.

Twenty minutes later, she found herself outside of Gallagher's pub with a tote bag full of groceries. It was now or never.

The doors were thrown open to encourage the warm sea breezes to come inside. Voices and laughter spilled from the pub and had Morgan pausing. If she went in there now, the whole village would know that she was asking Patrick to dinner. Her fingers ran across the scar on her palm again. Emboldened, she stepped through the entrance, scanning the cozy room until her eyes landed on Patrick. He was standing with Cait at the entrance to the kitchen.

Cait's eyes immediately found her and a wide smile crossed her face.

"Come over here! I haven't seen you in ages," Cait called and everyone turned to see who she was talking to.

Morgan nodded at all the regulars bellied up to the bar and hurried over to where Patrick stood. Her heart dropped as he nodded at her and then turned back to Cait.

"You were saying?"

Cait glared at him and turned, her arms open, to hug Morgan. Morgan smiled and returned the hug awkwardly, Cait's large belly pressing against her and getting in the way. A part of her wanted to scan Cait's womb and see what she was carrying.

"Don't you dare," Cait whispered into her ear and Morgan laughed.

"Sorry."

"Sorry about what?" Patrick said stiffly, having not been able to hear their conversation.

"Nothing, um, so I wanted to stop and see you," Morgan rushed out before she could talk herself out of saying anything.

"What for?" Patrick said stiffly and Morgan saw Cait's face go thunderous.

"I just, uh, wanted to see if you wanted to come over for dinner."

"That sounds like a date. I think it's best that we just be friends. Sorry, Morgan," Patrick said, his words clipped, as he turned his back and went into the storeroom.

A wave of shame washed over Morgan, and all of the lessons that she had learned in the past few days flew out the window.

"That ignorant idiot," Cait seethed, turning immediately to run her hands down Morgan's arms.

"No, no, it's fine, really," Morgan said, stepping back from Cait. Cait held her arm, keeping her there.

"No, it is not fine. Just because his pride is hurt doesn't mean he shouldn't give you another chance. Stupid man," Cait bit out, so angry she could barely speak.

"No, I should have expected this. People never stay with me once they realize how difficult I am. It's fine." Morgan ripped her arm from Cait's hand and hurried from the pub, keeping her gaze on the floor, desperately wishing that she had just stuck with her instinct about curling up on her couch with a good book.

She refused to cry.

Not over him, at least. It wasn't worth it. They'd barely established a relationship as it was.

And it just proved her point.

Relationships were complicated, full of minefields and messy emotions. It was best that she continued on alone.

Chapter Seventeen

THAT WOMAN, PATRICK thought. That woman was insane if she thought that he was going to fall into her trap again. All she did was lure him in and then push him away when he got too close. He was done getting his head chewed off for doing nothing wrong. Patrick paced, trying to cool the anger that burned in him, scanning the shelves, looking for something to organize.

The door flew open with a bang.

Patrick turned and pointed a finger at Cait. "Don't you dare start with me. This is none of your business."

"It happens in my pub, then it's my business," Cait said, raising her chin at him.

"Fine, then I quit," Patrick said, furious with her, furious with the lot of them. He made to push past her, but Cait wouldn't move.

Patrick couldn't very well push his pregnant boss, so he stepped back and crossed his arms, looking up at the ceiling.

"You most certainly will not quit, Patrick, what with me about to be giving birth any day now. What kind of man are you?"

Her words stung with the truth, and he hung his head, knowing she was right.

"Fine, I don't quit. But stay out of my business."

"I will not. What in the heck is wrong with you?" Cait yelled at him and Patrick whipped his head up, staring at her in surprise. Cait's cheeks were flushed and her eyes snapped in anger.

"Me? Me!" Patrick said, his hands on his hips as he towered over his boss.

"Yes, you! She finally works up the courage to ask you for dinner and you said no! What were you thinking?"

"Maybe I'm sick of being attacked every time I try to make a move with her. She's warm, then cold, warm, then cold. It makes no sense. Everything I try, I get slapped back for," Patrick said.

"Have you ever thought about the fact it is because of her past?"

Patrick threw up his hands and began to pace the room.

"Seeing as how nobody will tell me her past, I can't rightly know that now, can I?"

"You know she's an orphan," Cait said.

"So what's that got to do with it?"

Cait let out a high screech, like a tea kettle emitting steam and Patrick stopped, staring at her.

"Just think outside of yourself for once, would you? Orphans. They've never had love. They don't have a lot of relationships. They've never had anyone stand for them...or stay by their side. Her coming here was a huge risk on her part and you did exactly what every single person in her life has done – pushed her away. Nice job," Cait said scathingly.

Patrick's heart plummeted and he stared at Cait as thoughts whirled through his mind.

"So, my rejection of her just proved what she's always known? That people don't stick?"

"Pretty much," Cait said, her face tense.

"Shit, shit, shit," Patrick swore and paced.

"Well, what are you doing? Go get her," Cait ordered and Patrick straightened.

"You think?"

Cait turned as Shane came up behind her and wrapped his arms around her belly. She leaned back into him and closed her eyes a little with a small smile.

"Shane, where does Morgan live?"

Shane recited the address and then looked down at Cait and back to Patrick.

"Why?"

"I have to go to her," Patrick said.

Cait straightened and snagged a bottle of wine from the shelf next to her.

"Here. Take this. On the house. Now, don't screw it up," Cait called over her shoulder as Patrick pushed past her.

"I'm off the rest of the night," Patrick called back.

"I figured as much," Cait grumbled and then turned, her hands on her hips to survey her husband.

"Looks like you're pouring pints," she said with a smile. He leaned down and brushed his lips over hers.

"Yes, ma'am."

Chapter Eighteen

MORGAN CURSED HERSELF the entire walk, well run, home. As she huffed up the hill to her apartment she glared at anyone who dared to smile at her. What had she been thinking? Morgan had been on a high after her time with Fiona, thinking with hope for her future for once.

The cold slap of rejection was enough to bring her head out of the clouds. She should have expected this. Never in her life had someone stuck by her side. It was the reason she refused to get into relationships, Morgan reminded herself as she pounded up the worn wooden steps of her building. It would be best if she just kept her head down, worked hard, and didn't socialize much. Eventually she'd save enough money for her to move on to the next town.

Morgan slammed the bag of food on the counter and trailed her hand over the smooth countertop. Turning, she looked around at her little space. Damn it, she thought. It would be hard to leave this. Battling back the sadness that threatened to overtake her, Morgan systematically put the food away, refusing to waste anything even in her sorrow. She could eat on these groceries for the rest of the week.

The rest of the week, Morgan thought. Straightening, she crossed her arms and paced across her apartment. That would be how she would take it then. One week at a time. She'd grow her savings and in a few months, pick a new place and keep moving. Which was stupid, Morgan thought, because she'd finally put down roots.

A loud buzz caused her to shriek and she turned, one hand over her heart and the other over her mouth. The buzz continued incessantly and Morgan's eyes tracked the apartment, trying to find the cause of it.

"An intercom?" she said, rushing to a small box by the door that she had never seen before. It appeared she needed to pay more attention to her surroundings, she thought.

The buzz continued, grating against her ears, so she ran to the door, and leaned her cheek against it, pressing her ear to hear anything on the outside. She pressed the button once.

The buzzing stopped.

Morgan waiting, straining to hear anything.

The buzz made her jump again and she stepped back, realizing that there was another button on the intercom. She pressed it down, and spoke hesitantly into it.

"Hello?"

Morgan heard the door slam below and the pounding of steps on the stairs. She jumped back and smoothed her hair, realizing that she had inadvertently pressed the button to release the lock on the door in the lobby of the building.

Morgan struggled through a breath as she waited, knowing it was Patrick, and not knowing what to do. She'd never had a man in her space before, let alone a large, angry, testosterone-filled man.

A knock at the door made her jump. Morgan stood there, considering her choices.

"If you don't open this door I swear to God, I will kick it in," Patrick cursed outside the door and Morgan fumbled with the latch, pulling the door in.

Her eyes tracked to Patrick's face, and she was immediately lost. He looked wonderful, she thought in surprise. His eyes were bright with anger, his cheeks flushed, and his hair was mussed in a way that made her want to run her hands through it. Nervous, she licked her bottom lip as she watched him, unsure what to say.

"I brought wine," Patrick said, and Morgan looked down at his hand, a bottle clutched there.

"Um," Morgan said, and then wanted to kick herself for not having something suave or cool to say. It crossed her mind that she should send him packing for the way he had treated her at the pub.

"Aw, the hell with this," Patrick said. He pushed past Morgan and placed the bottle on the counter. Turning, he kicked the door closed and grabbed Morgan around the waist.

In seconds, Morgan was pressed to the door, with a very angry, very passionate man holding her to it. All of her senses went on alert at once and she froze, paralyzed from wanting him…scared of taking this next step.

Patrick lowered his mouth to within inches of hers. Looking up from beneath his lids, he pinned her with his gaze.

"I'm going to kiss you now. And I'm not going to stop," he breathed.

Heat flashed through Morgan and she struggled to remember Fiona's lesson. *The switch, picture the switch*, she screamed at herself. Moments before Patrick's lips touched hers, she slammed the switch to off in her brain.

And her world opened up.

Feeling free for the first time in her life, Morgan wrapped her arms around Patrick, digging her hands into his thick hair, and kissed him back with all of the exuberance and inexperience that she had. Moaning into her mouth, Patrick slid his hands down to her legs and cupping her butt, he lifted her until her legs were wrapped around him and she was pressed to a very hard, and very manly part of him.

Unable to help herself, Morgan squirmed against him, relishing in these new feelings that he was creating in her body. His lips continued to caress hers, his tongue expertly dipping into her mouth to play with hers.

Morgan broke the kiss and clasped his face in her hands. They stared at each other, inches apart, their breath coming in ragged bursts.

"I thought you just wanted to be friends," Morgan gasped out.

"I've never wanted to be friends with you, Morgan," Patrick said, his stare intense.

"What do you want?" Morgan whispered, trailing her hands over his arms, amazed at how strong he was. He lifted her like she weighed nothing, holding her imprisoned between his arms.

"It's been you. Since the moment that I saw you at Keelin's wedding. That first dance…that everything. I haven't looked at another girl since. It's been killing me to get closer to you," Patrick gasped out, his arousal and need evident for her both in his words and his hard length pressed between her legs.

"Oh, oh God, Patrick, I want you too, I just –" Morgan's words were cut off by Patrick's mouth and he seduced her slowly with his lips, his hands caressing her cheeks, his body pressed tight to hers.

Gasping, Morgan broke the kiss, scared she would get pulled too far under, not knowing how she would ever stop something that felt so good. Part of her wanted to bury her face in his neck and have him just hold her.

"You want me," Patrick said, his voice low with need and anger.

"I do. But, I just, Patrick, I've never done this before," Morgan rushed out and Patrick's eyes flashed to hers.

"Never done what, to be exact?" Patrick said carefully.

"This, relationships, kissing, sex, all of it," Morgan rushed out and then closed her eyes, heat creeping up her cheeks.

"You're a virgin?" Patrick asked, incredulous.

"Yes, and you're my first kiss at that," Morgan whispered, her eyes closed, refusing to look at him.

"Well that explains a lot," Patrick mused and Morgan's eyes shot open.

"What do you mean by that?"

"Just why you were so skittish with me. I was certain you didn't like me," Patrick said, a wide smile growing across his face. He looked like a cat that had just licked a bowl of cream.

"Why is this so funny?" Morgan demanded, glaring at him.

"It's not funny. It's amazing and wonderful and you're mine, all mine," Patrick crowed out as he pulled her away from the door and did a little spin with her in his arms. Morgan went a little dizzy as he set her down, her body sliding down his. Placing her hands on her hips, she glared up at him.

"Who says I'm yours? You're making a big assumption here," Morgan said, feeling grumpy for some reason.

"I say. But now I know that I'll have to take it slow with you. It will be fun to introduce you to all sorts of...pleasures," Patrick said, trailing his finger down Morgan's neck to brush it across her nipple. Morgan jerked and swallowed.

"Patrick, I don't know how to do this and I am not just talking sex." She batted his hand away from her breast, where heat was trailing through her body and her nipples were standing at attention, begging to be touched.

Patrick stepped back, his hands raised, a wicked smile on his face.

"Okay, so you don't know how to be in a relationship? Let's talk about it. Over dinner. I believe you were going to cook for me?"

Morgan huffed out a breath, not sure what to do, knowing that for some reason he annoyed her and attracted her at the same time. This must be what love was like, she thought.

"I may or may not cook for you," Morgan said, her nose in the air.

"You will. Because I've been on my feet all day and haven't eaten. You wouldn't want me to starve, would you?" Patrick asked, his voice pleading and charming at the same time.

Morgan huffed again and turned, a smile on her face as she dug into the contents of her fridge.

"Well, be warned, it's my first time cooking as well. So, I may kill you," Morgan said as she pulled the package of ground beef out and the other ingredients for a tomato sauce.

Patrick wandered closer and looked down at the ingredients.

"Spaghetti and meatballs? Perfect. I'm good at this one, we'll do it together," he said, feeling warm and bright and just so male next to her.

Together, Morgan thought.

There was a first for everything.

Chapter Nineteen

HOURS LATER, MORGAN felt like her face was stretched from smiling so much. Patrick sat close to her on the loveseat, and he'd pulled her legs over his lap. A warm glow from the wine dulled the edge of her anxiety, and she couldn't remember when she'd had a better night.

"Thank God I was here to cook, you'd have started the whole place on fire," Patrick commented, teasing a laugh from Morgan.

"I would not have," Morgan said, smacking him lightly on the arm.

"Sure and I know the smell of burning meat now, don't I?" Patrick raised an eyebrow at her outrageously and Morgan giggled, biting her lip.

"The meatballs turned out just fine," she said staunchly.

Patrick ran his fingers over her ankle, sending heat shooting up her leg. She tried to focus on what he was saying.

"I'll have to teach you how to make a fine Irish stew," Patrick mused, continuing his hypnotic rub of her feet. "You can make one pot and eat off it all week."

"I'd like that. It's just me here so if I can save money on groceries, it makes sense," Morgan said.

"Is money tight?" Patrick asked, tilting his head to look at her. Morgan lost herself for a moment in his eyes. He was just so handsome, she thought.

"It's better than it's ever been." Morgan batted the question away.

"Were things rough growing up?"

And just like that, Morgan felt her walls go up. Damn it, she cursed herself. *This is what people do in relationships*, she reminded herself. *They share about their pasts.*

Shrugging, Morgan pulled her feet from Patrick's grasp.

"I was in and out of foster homes. Money was never easy to come by and I never really had anything extra or a home of my own. This," she gestured to the studio, "is the first home that I can call my own. Aside from my van, that is."

Uncomfortable with the subject and wishing that they could go back to laughing about easy topics, Morgan stood and moved to her small kitchen. She braced her hands on the side of the sink as she waited for the water to warm.

"I lost you there, didn't I?"

Patrick's voice came from right behind her and Morgan jumped a bit. She dashed a quick smile over her shoulder and began to scrub the pot.

"It's fine. It isn't my favorite subject to talk about is all."

"I'm sorry," Patrick said simply.

Morgan shrugged again and berated herself for making a big deal of it.

"It's nothing. Can't change the past." She rinsed the pot and reached for a plate. "You had a big family?" Though she knew the answer, Morgan thought it was best to keep the conversation off of her and on him.

A beat of silence greeted her and then a sigh.

"Yes, a big loving family. There's nine of us total, not counting my parents," Patrick said from behind her and Morgan stiffened. Turning, she looked at him, her mouth hanging open.

"Nine? Nine brothers and sisters? You seemed like you came from a big family, but, wow," Morgan said, mentally trying to wrap her head around having to meet and remember eleven members of his family.

"Well there's more now as most are married and have kids. I'm the baby." Patrick grinned at her and Morgan groaned.

"Perfect, just perfect," she muttered and turned to scrub viciously at the plate.

"You'll have to meet them sometime," Patrick offered.

Morgan continued to grumble into the sink.

She jumped when Patrick's arms slipped around her waist from behind.

"They'll love you," Patrick said, his lips hot at her neck.

"Maybe," Morgan said, noncommittally. She highly doubted they would love her but she would put that thought on the backburner until she actually had to meet them.

"Why don't you put those dishes down so I can repay you for dinner." Patrick's mouth was at her neck and she shivered at the meaning in his words.

Carefully placing the dish back in the sink, Morgan did her mental off-switch routine before turning to face Patrick. She opened up her senses and scanned him with her mind, while she lost herself in his eyes. For all of the edge and stubbornness he had, Patrick had a kind heart. And, his need for her bordered on desperate.

Morgan slid her hands up Patrick's arms before hooking them around his neck and pulling her body tight against his. She wished that she could be some brazen seductress but instead she'd have to settle for brushing her lips across his and hoping that he would lead her.

And lead her he did. Morgan moaned against Patrick's lips as he hefted her again, sliding his arms beneath her thighs to hold her tight to his body. Slowly, he backed from the kitchenette until his knees hit the bed, his lips never leaving hers. Morgan gasped against his mouth, ravenous for more, a need clawing through her that she didn't know how to deal with.

"I want...I want," Morgan said against his lips, not knowing what she wanted, only knowing that she didn't want him to stop.

Patrick eased down on the bed with Morgan now straddling him. The position provided her with intimate knowledge of his lust, and she ground herself against his hard length, craving his nearness.

"Shhh," Patrick laughed at her and then rolled, dislodging Morgan so she lay on her back on the bed, bracing his arms around her head.

"Patrick," Morgan said, struggling to breathe easily.

"Let me," Patrick ordered and trailed one hand down her side until he reached the bottom of her shirt. He tugged a little and Morgan realized what he was asking. Nervous, but excited just the same, Morgan lifted herself and pulled the shirt over her head, and made quick work of her pants as well. She propped herself on her arms, suddenly feeling like she wanted to hide, and pulled her long hair to hide the plain white bra that covered her breasts.

"Beautiful," Patrick whispered, reaching out to still her hands. He tucked her hair behind her shoulders and traced his finger across the strap of her bra. "You have no idea what you do to me."

"Really?" Morgan said, pleasure and a newfound confidence seeping through her. "I wish that I had sexier underwear or something."

Patrick laughed and closed his eyes for a second.

"Trust me, plain white can be really hot. It's really sexy on you. I'm barely holding back here," Patrick said, continuing to toy with the strap of her bra, his eyes on hers.

Morgan reached behind for the clasp of her bra.

"Show me…show me how you feel," she whispered, unclasping the bra and pulling it from her body.

"Sweet Jesus," Patrick breathed and reached out with both his hands to cup her breasts. Morgan jumped as his thumbs brushed across her sensitive nipples and on a curse, Patrick crushed his mouth to hers.

She was lost, so lost, Morgan thought as she fell into a spiral of heat and emotion. Her body seemed fluid and warm under his touch, her mind so completely focused on the sensations he was pulling from her that she didn't once worry about if anything in her apartment was levitating. A coil of heat seemed to form low in her stomach, and she moved her hips against Patrick's, knowing she wanted him to touch her more.

"You're so beautiful," Patrick murmured against her lips as he slowed his caress on her breasts and pulled back to look at her.

"Thank you, you're really handsome too," Morgan said awkwardly and then blushed.

Patrick laughed and toyed with the waistband to her underwear, his eyes tracing her body again before coming back to meet hers.

"I want to touch you everywhere," Patrick said softly, heat lacing his words.

Morgan gulped as her mouth went dry. She nodded, nerves tingling up her back.

"Lie back," Patrick ordered and pushed Morgan gently back onto the bed. He moved to lie propped on one arm, staring down at her.

"I'm going to go slow and if you want to stop, just tell me," Patrick said, nuzzling into her neck and nipping at a sensitive spot there that sent shivers down her back.

"Okay," Morgan said.

"Close your eyes," Patrick said and Morgan looked at him with concern.

"Why?" she stuttered.

"Because I want you to feel. Just feel," Patrick said softly, bringing his lips to her face, kissing her eyes closed.

Morgan closed her eyes, trying to do what he said. Thoughts ping-ponged through her mind. Where would he touch next? Should she touch him back?

"Morgan."

Her eyes shot open as she squinted up at him.

"What?"

"Relax. You're scrunching your whole face up to keep your eyes closed." He laughed at her and Morgan felt herself relaxing.

"Oh, sorry." She smiled and closed her eyes, letting the tension release from her face. With her eyes closed, her senses were heightened and when Patrick brushed his hand across her nipple again, she moaned.

And jerked when he replaced his hand with his mouth.

"Oh, oh my," Morgan said, as a new and decidedly delicious sensation rippled through her as he kissed her breasts, licking gently at her nipples.

Unable to help herself, Morgan arched her back, loving the feelings that Patrick was sending through her body. He continued to kiss her breasts as he slid a hand under the waistband of her underwear. Morgan stiffened involuntarily and then relaxed as Patrick kept his hand still, just lightly toying with her waistband. Morgan wondered why he didn't keep going. Craving more, almost desperate to know what these sensations inside of her were demanding, Morgan lifted her hips to move Patrick's hand further down onto her.

Patrick chuckled against her breasts and Morgan wanted to scream. She needed something, anything, to release this ball of tension that had formed low in her belly.

"Please," Morgan gasped out, unable to articulate what it was that she wanted, but knowing that it was probably the elusive orgasm that everyone always talked about. It wasn't like she'd been hiding in a bush all these years at school. She'd just never had the opportunity to experience it.

Nor had she ever trusted someone enough to touch her this way.

Morgan moaned as Patrick slid his hand lower to find her slick with heat. The lust in her belly kicked up about ten notches and Morgan found herself writhing, desperately aching for release, before Patrick finally slipped his fingers inside of her and took her over the edge with one nudge.

A beautiful wave of heat and release washed through her, slamming her back to the bed as pure joy rocketed through her. It felt like all of her nerve endings fired at once and Morgan shouted out, unable to contain her joy in the moment. It was so crystalline and perfect, she wanted to bottle it and sell it at the store.

Morgan opened her eyes to find Patrick smiling down at her, a very satisfied look on his face.

"Thank you," Morgan said, smiling up at him.

"I think you needed that," Patrick said, leaning down to brush his lips over hers, before pulling his hand from her underwear. He sat up and checked the clock.

"I should be going," Patrick said.

Morgan sat up, crossing her arms over her breasts, to look at him in confusion.

"That's it? What about you? What about…the rest of it?" Morgan motioned with her hand, confused, not sure if she was being rejected.

Patrick leaned forward, his shoulders strong and wide over her, as he nibbled gently at her bottom lip.

"I want the rest of it. But I promised you that I would go slow. So, slow it will be," he said against her lips.

Morgan reached up to hook her arms around his neck, her bare breasts pushing into his chest, her sensitive nipples enjoying the contact.

"But, what about, you know, you?" Morgan said against his mouth.

"It won't be the first cold shower I've taken since I've met you," Patrick said and pulled her arms from around his neck to stand.

"Really?" Morgan said, intrigued by the thought of him lusting after her, a newly found confidence seeping through her.

"You don't have to look so delighted about it. Now, I know it's late and you've got to work in the morning. Can I take you to dinner…" Patrick paused and thought about it. "Sunday? Would Sunday work? I'm on close the rest of the week. You're welcome to come and keep me company at the pub though."

Morgan tilted her head and considered that.

"The village will gossip."

Patrick brushed a finger over her nose.

"They already are."

Chapter Twenty

MORGAN FOUND HERSELF humming the next morning as she stocked the display by the register with a new order of prints that had just arrived.

"Someone's in a good mood this morning," Aislinn commented as she came in from the back, her arms full of canvases.

"Here, let me help you," Morgan said, bypassing her comment.

She rushed to pull a few canvasses from Aislinn's arms, following her into the stock room and placing them on the shelves.

"Dodging the question." Aislinn turned to her as they left the stockroom.

Morgan blushed and Aislinn stopped, grabbing her arm.

"You had sex!"

"Oh my God," Morgan groaned and covered her face with her hands, shaking her head.

"Was it bad? Oh, if he messed this up, I swear that I will skin him alive," Aislinn muttered, pacing in front of Morgan. Morgan raised her hand weakly, torn between laughing or yelling at Aislinn.

"I did not have sex. What I did was have a first real date with a very kind, and sexy, man," Morgan said primly.

Aislinn narrowed her eyes at Morgan.

"We're talking about Patrick, right?"

"Yes!" Morgan exclaimed, swatting Aislinn with her hand. "Yes, oh, he's just so…I…" She found herself blushing again.

"Why, you're besotted," Aislinn said.

"I am certainly not," Morgan said stiffly, moving away from Aislinn with her nose in the air.

"Sure and I know what besotted looks like and from where I'm standing…you're besotted." Aislinn's steely voice followed Morgan into the showroom.

Morgan whirled and put her hands on her hips.

"And so what if I am?"

"Well, good for you. I encourage it," Aislinn said with an easy smile and Morgan laughed, the tension draining from her.

"We didn't sleep together. We just…" Morgan debated an appropriate way of discussing what they had done.

"Fooled around?" Aislinn offered.

Morgan pointed her finger at her boss, nodding.

"Yes, that. And it was lovely. And, he left like a gentleman, not trying to go any further. I…I've never felt like this before. Nervous, excited, scared," Morgan admitted.

Aislinn tucked her mass of curls over her shoulders and smiled at Morgan but she could see the worry in her boss's eyes.

"What?"

"Nothing, I worry about you because I know how powerful a first love can be. Everyone must go through it once. It's good for you," Aislinn said with a smile.

"First love? I'm not in love," Morgan protested, raising an eyebrow at Aislinn.

Aislinn raised her hands in defense.

"Sorry, wrong word then," she said with a smile. "That being said, Patrick's a solid guy. You could do far worse."

Morgan nibbled at her lip as she considered Aislinn's words.

"He doesn't know about me…about my abilities," she blurted out.

"Ah," Aislinn said.

"What should I do?" Morgan asked, nervously straightening a painting of the cove.

"Well, I'm a bit different than Cait and Keelin. I told Baird about me immediately. It took him a while to believe it, but I accept that part of myself. I always have. So, ultimately, it comes down to your comfort level in sharing your gift."

"I don't know if I can," Morgan said nervously.

"Then don't. But, I suspect that he will find out along the way if you date him for a while, so keep that in mind," Aislinn cautioned.

"He knows about Cait's abilities. I'm not sure who else's."

"Patrick's lived here for a long time. Very little probably surprises him when it comes to that stuff," Aislinn said.

"So you think he'll be receptive?"

"I can't presume to know the answer to that, Morgan. I think the real question is, can you accept yourself enough to not hide who you are?"

On those words, Aislinn swept from the room, leaving Morgan with some deep self-reflection.

"It can never be easy, can it," she muttered to herself as she found her cup of tea and sipped it, her mind returning to her time with Patrick last night. It *had* been easy, between them, she thought.

And maybe Aislinn was right. If being honest about who she was would form the foundation of their relationship, then it would seem like a pretty hurtful thing to do to hide it from him.

Morgan thought back to all of the brief relationships that she had had growing up. She didn't want to be that person anymore, she realized. Flitting from relationship to relationship, never forming bonds with people. Granted, she'd had no choice when the foster homes had returned her to the nuns, but ever since she'd runaway and been on her own, Morgan had refused to form real bonds with anyone.

Until Grace's Cove.

She had friends now, even, maybe the beginning of a family, Morgan thought as Fiona flashed through her mind.

Telling Patrick about her abilities wouldn't be the hardest thing she'd gone through in her life, she thought. Aislinn was right. Morgan was finally coming into her own. She didn't need to hide herself from those closest to her in her life. Coming to a resolution, Morgan smiled grimly. Now she just needed to find the right time to tell him.

Later that day, Morgan grimaced.

She hadn't thought that time would present itself so soon, she thought as she stared in shock at Patrick sitting on the front step of her building.

"I hadn't expected to see you," Morgan said, a smile flitting across her face.

He looked wonderful. A button-down shirt complemented his broad chest and his hair was delightfully mussed in the way that made her want to run her hands through it. She couldn't seem to get enough of looking at him.

She smiled even more broadly as he pulled his hand from behind his back and held a shopping bag up to her.

"What's this?" She tilted her head and looked up at him in question.

"Let me in and I'll show you," Patrick said with a smile.

"Oh, okay," Morgan said, her heart rate picking up a notch. A smile crossed Patrick's face and he leaned down to brush his lips against hers. Morgan leaned into him, craving the heat and security he brought.

"Guess you aren't worried about the village anymore, are you?" Patrick said, pulling back and waving at a passerby.

Morgan groaned as heat flashed over her cheeks and she pulled the door to her building open.

"Upstairs before you start a scandal," Morgan ordered and Patrick laughed at her, holding the door open for her.

They made quick work of the stairs and moments later, Morgan had her back to her door like the night before while Patrick kissed her senseless.

Pulling back, he ran a thumb over her lips.

"I have to stop before I get too distracted. Here, open your gift," Patrick ordered.

Morgan smiled shyly at him and moved to where the shopping bag sat on the counter, Peeking in, she spied a stock pot. Turning she raised an eyebrow at him.

"A pot?"

"Take the lid off."

Morgan lifted the lid and gaped down at the Irish stew in the pot.

"Stew? You brought me stew?"

"I cooked it myself. If you like it, I'll teach you to make it. I even got my mum to bake some brown bread for you."

At the mention of his mother, Morgan felt her nerves kick in again. Blowing out a breath, she turned to him.

"This is really sweet of you. You didn't have to do that," she began.

Patrick shrugged.

"I noticed that your refrigerator was empty last night. Now you don't have to think about dinner for a couple days until I can take you out on Sunday," he said with a smile and Morgan's heart cracked open a bit.

"That's really incredibly kind of you. Seriously, thank you. Um, hey, do you have a minute?" Morgan rushed out, worried that she would go too far down the road with Patrick, meet his family, form bonds, and then have him turn his back on her when he found out her secrets. It was now or never.

"Sure, I can spare a few before work."

Morgan reached out and grabbed his hand, pulling him to her loveseat so that he sat close to her. She needed to be near him so she could read his every reaction. If he lied to her…well, she was quite certain a piece of her would die.

"What's wrong?" Patrick asked, reaching out to trace his hand over her cheek.

"Okay, I just…I'm just going to say it and then you need to tell me how you feel," Morgan said, taking a deep breath and keeping her eyes locked on his.

"You're scaring me."

"I, it's just…okay, here goes." Morgan blew out a breath. "I have abilities…like Cait does and Fiona does."

There, she'd done it. She couldn't be accused of lying. Morgan sat back and watched him, waiting for any indication.

"Wait…like Cait? You can read minds? You can heal? Are you…a descendant?" Patrick asked, his eyes boring into hers.

Swallowing, Morgan nodded slowly, her eyes never leaving his. The silence stretched between them.

"Far out," Patrick said finally and Morgan felt like her heart would explode in her chest.

"Far out?" Morgan exclaimed.

"Sure, it's pretty cool. So what's your super power?" Patrick asked, trailing his hand down her arm and Morgan felt tears spring unbidden to her eyes.

"Hey, don't cry," Patrick said, leaning forward to capture her lips in a soft kiss.

"It's just, nobody's ever accepted me so easily before," Morgan gasped into his mouth, the tears coming faster, unable to stop the emotion that welled up inside of her.

"Shh, it's okay. As long as you aren't some dark arts crazy devil worshiper, I'm fairly certain that I can handle what you throw at me."

Morgan wondered how he would react if she lifted the couch they were sitting on. Nerves shot through her again and she decided that would be a secret that he didn't need to know. Now that she knew how to control that side of her, she never planned on using it again. Feeling comfortable with that decision, Morgan pulled back and cupped Patrick's face in her hands.

"You're a good man," she whispered.

"So, what can you do?" Patrick asked.

"A little bit of this…a little bit of that. I can kind of read minds, I'm sort of an empath, and I can kind of help with healing. I'm pretty much a mutt, actually," Morgan said.

"Cool, so what am I thinking right now?" Patrick said, leering at the V in her blouse. She laughed and swatted him lightly.

"I think that I could tell you that without having to read your mind."

Impulsively, she reached out and hugged him. Pressing her face into his neck, she mumbled, "Thank you."

"What's that?"

"Thank you. Thank you for sticking with me. For not freaking out about this, thank you," Morgan said, inhaling his scent as she wiped her tears away.

"I'm not going anywhere, Morgan," Patrick said.

Morgan leaned back and met his eyes.

"I think that I'm beginning to see that," she said softly.

"Good, don't forget it. Now, I have to go to work or Cait will fire me and I won't be able to buy you nice things and take you to fancy dinners," Patrick said with a smile and kissed her once more before rising.

Morgan lifted her chin.

"I don't need that stuff, Patrick," she said, knowing that he was probably on a bit of a budget as well.

"Yes, you do," Patrick said, stopping at her door to turn and wave. "And I'm the man to give it to you."

After the door closed, Morgan just stared at it for a while, knowing that she probably had a stupid grin across her face.

"Oh, dang it all. Besotted it is," she grumbled and stood up to put the soup in the fridge.

Aislinn was never wrong.

Chapter Twenty-One

THE DAYS UNTIL Sunday passed in a blur for Morgan. With spring weather came tourists, and the gallery had been hopping. Between working extra hours for Aislinn and trying to help Flynn where she could, Sunday arrived before she knew it.

Morgan stood in front of her closet, contemplating what to wear. She looked down at the deep red silk of her matching bra and underwear. She'd been paid on Friday and had taken a quick trip to the next town over to invest in a few new items for herself.

It had been fun, she thought. To buy clothes knowing she would wear them for someone.

She fingered a silky blouse that she had picked up on impulse. The vibrant purple and red hues of the pattern had sung to her, reflecting her current mood. Pulling it out, Morgan reached for her gray skinny jeans and favorite black pumps. Simple, but sexy, and dressy enough for any place that he would take her in town. She'd braided her hair half back again and now, all she had to do was wait.

Patrick had stopped at the gallery yesterday to tell her that he'd be picking her up at six, but had given her no indication of where he was taking her. He'd even been deliberately thinking about her body when she'd scanned his mind to see if she could get a clue.

And hadn't he caught her at that? Morgan huffed out a small laugh remembering how Patrick had waved his finger at her and called her naughty. He must have known she would try reading his mind.

The buzz at her door made her jump and Morgan grabbed her small purse before clattering quickly down the wooden stairs.

"Hi," she said, beaming at him. Patrick smiled down at her, looking handsome in a plaid button-down and gray khakis. His shoes shone and his hair looked slightly more tamed than usual. Morgan wanted to reach and muss it up for him.

"You look great," Patrick said, leaning down to kiss her.

"Thanks, I hope it is fine for where we are going," she said shyly, following him to his compact sedan parked in front of her building. A rusty brown, the car had seen better days. Patrick shrugged sheepishly.

"Sorry about the car. It's all I can afford at the moment."

Morgan smiled up at him as she eased herself into the seat. "Hey, you're talking to a girl who drives a thirty-year-old van. I get it."

Patrick closed the door, the hinges protesting with a squeak and Morgan blew out a breath, feeling relieved. She wasn't sure if she could have handled a rich guy sweeping her off her feet. It was nice that she and Patrick were on the same level.

"It won't be a long drive. We're going to the best place in town for dinner," Patrick said as he pulled away from the curb. "How's work been?"

Morgan wondered if he was changing the subject but smiled at him anyway and began to tell him about her busy days.

"Ah, the pub's been packed too. It's been good craic as we've had some great music. The tourist season has begun," he said as he pulled in front of a house.

"Patrick, where are we?" Morgan asked, as she stared at the house. It was a lovely brick house, with a cheerful green trim and bright blue flower boxes.

"Sunday dinner with the family," Patrick said, turning to smile at her.

Morgan's mouth gaped open and she worked to breathe as panic slammed into her.

"Patrick, I can't, I can't do family stuff…" Morgan began.

"Sure you can. They're easy. Trust me, you'll be fine," Patrick said easily and got out of the car, rounding it and opening the door.

Morgan forced herself to breathe normally, trying to quell the anxiety that threatened to overtake her. Families just weren't her thing, she thought.

Patrick opened the door and looked down at her expectantly.

"Patrick. I'm not good at this stuff," she whispered to him, making one last attempt to stop him.

"That's okay. You'll learn," he said easily and grasped her hand, pulling her from the car. She stood stiffly next to him, not sure what to do, just knowing that she would feel like an outcast.

"They're going to hate me," she whispered to him.

"No they won't. They love everyone. Plus, they'll be too busy running after the kids to pay you much mind."

Morgan gulped and stood at the door with him, wishing she was elsewhere.

"Well it's about time he brought you." A round woman held the door open, cheerfulness vibrating from every inch of her. Despite her nervousness, Morgan couldn't help but smile. With her dark curls and laughing gray eyes, Morgan could see where Patrick got his looks from.

"Mrs. Kearney, so nice to meet you," Morgan said automatically, holding her hand out.

Morgan jolted as she was crushed into a hug, and she nervously patted the woman's back.

"Feel free to call me Agatha," Mrs. Kearney said, pulling back to smile at her. "And aren't you just a picture. I've been dying to get to the gallery and meet you, but I've been over my head with work lately."

"What do you do?" Morgan said politely.

"She makes some of the finest lace this side of Ireland," Patrick said proudly, leaning over to kiss his mother's cheek.

"Ah, go on you," Agatha said, swatting her son lightly and slipping her arm through Morgan's. "Come back, you must meet everyone."

Morgan stiffened as Agatha began to lead her towards the back of the house where it sounded like a small crowd was talking and laughing. Spying a pile of lace on a long worktable, Morgan stopped.

"Is that yours?"

"Aye, I'm a bit behind."

"Do you mind if I see it?"

"Of course," Agatha said warmly and moved towards her work. Morgan stood by the table, astounded at the masterful work that came from this motherly woman. Placemats, table runners, and doilies were in small piles, packaged in clear cellophane. The lace was intricate and Morgan imagined it was painstaking to create.

"These are lovely. Where do you sell through? I'd love to have some of this at the gallery," Morgan said, running her fingers over a napkin.

"Really? I usually ship them up to Dublin, but it would save me some hassle to sell them here," Agatha said, beaming up at Morgan.

Morgan found herself liking Agatha, and wanted to help her.

"Of course. I can't imagine that Aislinn would have a problem with it. We'll have to discuss price and what you'd be willing to sell, but I really see these selling well. In fact, we could maybe offer a few other items from town." Morgan tapped her lip as she scanned the table again. "It could almost be a one-stop shop for local artisan crafts," she mused.

Agatha blushed. "Go on now, I'm not a fancy artist like Aislinn."

Morgan lifted the intricate lace napkin and held it in front of Agatha.

"This is art. You're blind if you can't see that. I suspect you are probably undercharging as well. The Dublin shops probably triple what you sell it to them for."

Agatha's mouth dropped open.

"I'd never thought of that."

"Don't worry. I'll make sure you charge what you're worth," Morgan said determinedly.

"Wow, Patrick, you've outdone yourself this time."

A booming voice from the back room brought her head up and Morgan blushed to see what looked like thirty people standing with their arms crossed, openly assessing her. Sweat broke out on her palms and she wiped them across her pants.

"Okay, enough everyone. Go back to getting dinner ready. You'll meet her one at a time," Patrick ordered and came to wrap his arm around Morgan's waist.

"She's shy, Mum," Patrick said, smiling down at Agatha.

"Of course, dear. Don't let the lot of them get to you. They all answer to me," Agatha said with a sniff before sweeping back to the kitchen. Morgan could hear her barking orders out to everyone and she grinned despite herself.

"Patrick, there are so many people. How will I remember their names?"

"Don't bother. You'll learn them eventually. For now, just relax and enjoy one of the best home-cooked meals you'll ever have," Patrick said and swept her along to the back room.

As people enveloped her, Morgan felt like the room around her was growing smaller. Heat licked up her spine and she tried to smile politely at all of the faces grinning at her.

This was going to be a nightmare, she thought.

Chapter Twenty-Two

AND SHE WASN'T far wrong, Morgan thought an hour later as they sat squished together at a long dining room table. Patrick's father, a striking image of what Patrick would look like when he was older, entertained with stories from his job in sales. Morgan hadn't even bothered trying to remember all of the siblings and their spouses who peered curiously at her over Agatha's Sunday ham.

Morgan sighed quietly and took another sip of her wine. His family had been nothing but inviting, but it was just so much to take in at once. The questions, the names, the way they interrupted each other and talked over each other. She did her best to keep quiet and follow the conversation and prayed for dinner to end early.

"So, tell us about your family, Morgan," a sister, Aileen, Morgan thought, said from across the table, her eyebrow raised in question. She was one of the younger ones, and a bit edgier. Morgan had kept her eye on her through dinner, expecting the worst.

"I don't have a family," Morgan said softly and then cringed as the entire dinner table went quiet. Patrick immediately wrapped his arm around Morgan's waist for support.

"What's that, dear?" said Patrick's dad, peering at her over his glasses.

"I, um, I don't have a family. I'm an orphan." Morgan shrugged and took a sip of her wine, praying the cool liquid would soothe her hot throat.

"How...interesting. I've heard you moved around a lot. What are you – a tinker or something?" Aileen smirked at her and Morgan felt the red sweep of anger rush over her. Calling someone a gypsy was no small insult, and the rest of the table gasped at Aileen.

"I'm not, thanks, excuse me, I must be going." Morgan shoved away from the table, hating that she was giving Aileen the show that she wanted, but she felt suffocated, unable to get her thoughts straight, and she needed air. She turned to Agatha.

"Thank you kindly for a nice dinner. I'm sorry that I won't be finishing it with you." With her back stiff, she turned and marched through the house, focused only on the freedom that the front yard offered her. A trill of laughter followed her and she caught Aileen's words..."Was it something I said?" just before she pushed outside, gasping for air, and desperately trying to control her impulse to dump Aileen's plate of food over her head.

Morgan paced the yard, rubbing her hands over her arms, and forced herself to calm down. It wasn't the first time she'd been made a fool of, she thought. She could handle this. So why did it hurt so much, Morgan thought as she sighed and began the walk back into the village, wishing that she had chosen flats instead of pumps.

"Morgan, wait, please." A voice sounded behind her.

Morgan turned, surprised to see that Agatha had followed her outside and not Patrick. Patrick was probably too embarrassed of her, she thought with a sniff and forced herself to tamp the anger down.

"I'm sorry. I know that it was rude of me to leave like that," Morgan said stiffly, looking over Agatha's shoulder.

Agatha came to a stop in front of her and reached up to pat Morgan's arm softly. Morgan turned and looked down at the round woman, desperately wishing to be anywhere else but there.

"You've nothing to apologize for. It's Aileen who needs to apologize. I'll say that I'm right sorry on her behalf. I've raised my children to be kinder than that. Patrick's always been her favorite brother and she's a might bit protective of him is all. But she overstepped her boundaries today and insulted a guest in our home and for that I'm sorry."

Morgan gaped down at this sweet woman, surprised that she was siding with Morgan.

"I…it's fine. Really, I'll live," Morgan said quickly.

"You're welcome in my home, anytime, with or without Patrick. I suspect that you could use some mothering in your life, and it comes naturally to me. I hope you'll stop by for a cup of tea sometime."

Morgan's heart warmed at her words and impulsively she bent down and hugged Agatha.

"I sure do appreciate that. I really would like to talk about getting your lace into the store."

"Come by this week. We'll talk. I'll make sure it's just you and me. No bother. Or perhaps I can come to the gallery? I haven't been there since you've taken over management."

"I'd like that," Morgan said with a smile and then looked up at the sound of the door closing behind her.

"Patrick, you need to take Morgan home. Or for a nice walk as the sun sets," Agatha called behind her, knowing who stood at the door without looking.

"I'm going to, Mum. I just had to give Aileen a stern talking to is all."

Patrick stomped towards them, anger radiating from his every movement. Morgan felt her back go up and wasn't sure what to do.

"She's not allowed at any more Sunday dinners," Patrick said furiously down to his mother.

"I'll talk to her, Patrick. I've already told Morgan how sorry I am."

Patrick finally turned and saw the sheen of tears in Morgan's eyes. He cursed and shook his head, before bending to kiss his mother's cheek.

"We'll talk this week," he said and reached around his mother to grab Morgan's arm and drag her towards the car. Morgan went, mainly because she didn't relish walking back into town in her heels. She wasn't sure if she would be able to handle the messy emotional scene that was about to come and she put her walls up to protect herself in advance.

Patrick didn't say a word as he started the car and pulled away from the house, while Morgan stared out of the window, her body turned away from him.

"You don't have to act like I've beat you," Patrick shouted after a few moments of silence and Morgan jumped, her hand trembling in surprise.

"I'm not," Morgan said, glaring at him.

"Sure and you are! You're all but curled up in a ball, turned away from me. What gives?"

Morgan felt her eyes growing wider as she stared him down. He pulled the car into a spot in front of her apartment.

"Thanks for a great dinner. Let's never do it again," Morgan seethed at him and slammed the car door, all but running to her door.

"Oh no you don't," Patrick shouted and followed her through the door, pounding up the steps to her apartment after her.

"I didn't invite you up," Morgan said, standing at her door with the key in the lock, her chest heaving, anger pounding through her.

"You're not pushing me away again, not this time," Patrick swore and grabbed her hand, turning the key and shoving her inside. Morgan almost tripped over her feet as she was pushed through the door and then turned, her mouth gaping open at him, as Patrick slammed the door and locked it, blocking her way out.

"Excuse me, but who do you think you are? This is my space. Mine! You don't get to say who comes in here. I do. My space. Just leave me alone!" Morgan shrieked, surprising even herself with the ferocity of her words.

"So it's like that then? Every time you get upset, you'll just shut me out? Run away and hide in your space?" Patrick shouted back at her, equally as angry.

"You don't get it! You don't get what it's like for me, Patrick!" Morgan screamed at him and then turned, hating that this was happening, hating that they were going down the road that she had imagined they would.

"Then tell me, damn it. Make me understand!" Patrick shouted, desperation in his voice. Morgan closed her eyes, hearing under the anger and hurt his kindness and love. He really wanted to know.

And it was her fault that she hadn't let him in.

Morgan took a few deep breaths, trying to force her anger down so she could speak. Walking further into her apartment, she reached her bed and sat down, finally raising her eyes to look at Patrick.

He stood by the door, his arms crossed, his skin flushed, his eyes never leaving her. And in that moment, Morgan felt her heart crack open completely. She knew that she loved him then. It washed over her in a way that nothing had before, leaving her warm, scared, and for the first time, seeing Patrick with new eyes. This was a man she could be with. Not just date or have fun with, but really be with, she thought.

"So, I know you thought you were doing well tonight…because hey, what girl doesn't want to be taken home to the family? But it was too much for me. All of them, all at once like that…it was, God, it kind of felt like back when I walked into a foster home for the first time. The family would stare me down, ask questions, judge me. It was never a good experience for me. I guess that I've just built up a lot of anxiety around that type of experience." Morgan shrugged, pleading with her eyes for Patrick to understand her.

"Aww, shit," Patrick cursed and moved forward to come sit next to her on the bed. "I didn't even think of that. You never talk about it. I didn't think it would be a big deal."

Morgan turned and looked at him, a small smile on her face.

"And it wouldn't be a big deal. For most people. But it was for me. It…it was hard for me growing up. Up until I was sixteen, it was a blur of homes, and being back with the nuns. I never stayed longer than nine months with a family. Once they found out about...well, you know," Morgan pointed at her head, "they would send me packing. I got used to putting my walls up, never forming attachments, and expecting that I would be rejected. Never being good enough was pretty much the norm for me. I was never good enough, funny enough, smart enough...for any family. Nobody wanted me."

Morgan blinked back the tears that came to her eyes and tried to tamp down on the emotions of shame and anxiety that surfaced in her at the thoughts. She rubbed her finger over the scar on her palm for strength.

"Well..." Patrick began and Morgan raised her hand to cut him off.

"And I was abused."

"What?" Patrick said, a dark cloud of fury moving across his handsome features.

"Not like you are thinking. But it was abuse in its own way. Something that Baird is helping me to see," Morgan said with a rueful smile. "The nuns and the priest, well they liked to perform an exorcism on me fairly regularly. They'd tie me to the bed and you know..." Morgan trailed off at the scary expression on Patrick's face.

"They exorcised you? You were just a little girl!" Patrick said, biting the words out between tight lips.

"It's okay, really. They thought they were doing best," Morgan said automatically and then stopped, again raising her hand to silence Patrick. "Actually, it's not okay. I get that now. They were wrong. There's nothing evil or wrong about me. I'm working on accepting that," she said softly.

Patrick turned and ran his hand down her cheek, his touch as gentle as the brush of a butterfly's wing.

"Thank you for telling me. I understand more now. I hope you can see that you have a home with me, in my heart. That I think you are beautiful, and brilliant, and I want to see you fly. I will protect you, so long as you trust me and are faithful to me, I'll be by your side," Patrick said fiercely, love and light shining in his eyes.

Morgan's heart did a little spin in her chest and then she fell into his arms, tears running down her neck as she nuzzled her face into his neck.

"Nobody's been there for me," Morgan said, pressing her face into his shoulder, loving when his strong arms came around her, lifting her until she pressed tightly against his hard body.

"I am. I promise," Patrick said and then his lips found hers, kissing away the tears that seeped over them, his love pouring into her.

Morgan pulled back and grabbed his hand, bringing it to her chest. She searched his eyes with hers.

"I want you to love me. Please, Patrick. Show me what love is," she whispered.

Patrick swallowed.

"You're sure? I can take it slow, we don't have to do this now," he said softly, his light eyes awash with concern.

"I know," Morgan said simply and smiled gently at him. She'd never been more certain of a decision in her life.

"It would be my honor," Patrick said and Morgan grinned at the formality of his words.

"Then I'd like to belong to you," Morgan said and Patrick groaned, leaning forward to nip at her lip.

She gasped as he lifted her and turned, laying her down on the bed. The warm light of the setting sun shone through her window, casting the bed in a golden glow that seemed to highlight the moment. Morgan watched as Patrick stood and quickly stripped, gaping at the ridge of muscles that ran down his stomach before disappearing into his boxer briefs. She gulped at the hard length contained therein, wondering how it would feel. Would he hurt her?

"It'll be okay," Patrick said, following her eyes and then flashing her a wicked smile full of promise that had her insides heating.

"I…I got something for you," Morgan said shyly as he moved back to the bed. Patrick put his hands at his waist and tilted his head at her.

"Oh?"

Morgan smiled up at him and then sat up, pulling her loose blouse easily over her head and quickly divesting herself of her skinny jeans. She knelt on the bed, looking up at him hopefully.

"Dear lord," Patrick said, his eyes taking in her matching red silk bra and underwear.

"You like?"

"Yes. Oh you meant the underwear? Yeah, that's nice too." Morgan chuckled and mock smacked him on the shoulder as he rolled onto the bed, snagging her with his arm to roll her under him.

"Hey, I spent a long time picking this out," she said, gasping with laughter as his lips descended on hers.

"And I'll spend a long time taking it off you," he murmured and kissed his way down her throat, trailing heat, until his mouth found her nipple through the silk. Morgan moaned and arched her back into him, marveling at this new sensation of wet silk against her skin.

Patrick continued his relentless assault of her breasts while running his hand down her side, trailing goosebumps in his wake. Morgan didn't know what to do with her hands; she wanted to touch him, feel him, be a part of him. Raising her arms, she trailed her hands over his shoulders, marveling at the divets and ridges of his muscles. She stroked his back, pulling him down to her, enjoying the weight of him, the overwhelming manliness of his body hovering over hers.

Morgan gasped as he pulled back and stroked her over her lace panties.

"That feels good," she said softly, nibbling at his shoulder with her mouth.

"I'm going to get you ready for me; just lie back and enjoy this," Patrick said with a smile and continued to stroke her through the silk. Morgan moaned as heat whipped through her, building in a tight coil low in her stomach. She gasped out, wanting more.

"Let go, love," Patrick instructed and Morgan did just that, slipping easily over the edge into a spiral of pleasure that sucked her down as Patrick slid off her underpants and positioned himself between her legs.

"You're going to do it now?" Morgan asked, bracing herself.

Patrick laughed at her, bending to bite at the soft flesh of her inner thigh.

"Not quite yet, soon though," he said and Morgan jumped as he kissed his way up her thigh before finding her with his mouth.

"Oh, oh my." Morgan moaned and arched into him, helpless to control herself as the sensations he teased from her with his tongue whipped through her and sent her careering sharply off the cliff into a wave of pleasure.

Morgan sat up and reached for him, pulling him to her so she could kiss him. She tasted herself on his mouth and it only heightened her pleasure. Patrick broke the kiss and Morgan looked up at him in confusion. He sat back on his heels and reached for a foil packet, holding it up to her.

"Protection. Unless you're on the pill?" he asked.

"No, God, no. I didn't even think about it. Thank you," Morgan said, smiling up at him, knowing that she wouldn't have been able to stop even if they didn't have protection and grateful that they hadn't had to face that choice.

Patrick moved between her legs again, and she met his eyes.

"You're mine," he whispered, bending to trace his lips over hers. Morgan gasped as she felt him, and then he kissed her deeply, causing her to focus on him and not his sudden entrance into her body. Pain quickly gave way to pleasure and Morgan laughed into his mouth as Patrick brought her swiftly into womanhood, claiming her as his forever.

A while later, Morgan took in the new joy of sharing her bed with a man. They lay curled together under her comforter, her head resting on his chest.

"That was wonderful. Should we do it again?" Morgan asked hopefully and she felt his chuckle rumble through his chest.

"I suspect you'll be sore. We'll have plenty of time to practice," Patrick said, pressing his lips to her hair.

"This is nice," Morgan said sleepily against his chest.

"I know. I should probably go though," Patrick said.

Morgan propped herself up on her hands, looking searchingly down into his eyes.

"Stay," she asked. The first time she had ever asked someone to stay in her life, she thought.

Patrick seemed to sense the urgency behind her words and nodded.

"I'd like that."

Chapter Twenty-Three

PATRICK WHISTLED AS he unpacked boxes of liquor and stocked the shelves. He was at the pub far earlier in the day than usual, and he had Morgan to thank for that. He supposed they would have to get used to working on different schedules, but it was nothing that a cup of coffee couldn't fix.

He'd never met someone like Morgan before. Stunningly beautiful, completely unaware of it, and surprisingly vulnerable. It had been his experience that most beautiful women knew it and often used it to their advantage. It was a breath of fresh air to be with someone who was so unaware of her own power.

Power, Patrick thought as he stocked a bottle of Jameson's. Though it had surprised him when she'd told him of her extra abilities, it was nothing that he hadn't dealt with before. He already knew about Cait's ability and was fairly certain Aislinn had something going on as well. And there was no denying the whispers of Fiona's great healing powers. It was just a part and parcel of the rhythm and flow of village life. Morgan would fit seamlessly in if she would just let herself.

He wished that she would come to the pub more. Most of the women who were jealous of her beauty would see that Morgan was just shy. If only she would open up a little more, Patrick was certain that Morgan would be accepted by the villagers and would start to feel like this was home.

And wasn't that his biggest fear?

Patrick stilled and thought about it. Morgan was a runner, and she'd been on her own for a long time. He was happy that she was putting down roots here.

He'd just have to do his best to convince her to stay.

Smiling, he went back to work and planned his next way to surprise Morgan.

"You had sex." Cait's accusatory voice caused him to jump and he turned to glare at her.

"Would you just?" Patrick said, cursing softly under his breath and trying to bring his heart rate down.

Cait waddled into the room, her hand unconsciously rubbing the large mound of her belly until she was close enough to poke Patrick in the arm.

"You did. I know."

"Would you stop reading my mind?"

"Please. You're here hours earlier than you should be and you are whistling like a canary bird freed from its cage. I know the signs."

Patrick sighed and wiped his hand over his face.

"Yes, I did. And it was wonderful and she's wonderful and I will do everything in my power to make her happy. Okay?" Patrick said.

Cait measured him with one long glance.

"Okay."

"That's it? No interrogation?"

"No. You know I'll find you and kill you if you hurt her so I'm good with it."

Patrick rolled his eyes at his boss's retreating back.

"Shouldn't you be more focused on having that baby?"

"I'm not due for a few more days."

"Saturday works for me," Patrick called after her and laughed as she flung a middle finger into the air before shutting him into the stock room.

Chapter Twenty-Four

MORGAN HUMMED AS she ran through the numbers from the week before. If they had another week like this, she'd encourage Aislinn to take out some advertising on some of the travel websites. Making a note to contact a few sites for pricing, Morgan glanced up when the bells above the door tinkled.

Just lovely, she thought and then pasted a polite smile on her face as Aileen and Agatha wandered through the gallery to where she stood.

Aileen's cheeks had a slight flush to them and she offered Morgan a sheepish smile. Agatha poked her in the back.

"I know, Mum, I was going to come here either way, you know," Aileen said, glaring over her shoulder at Agatha before turning back to Morgan.

"Can I help you with something?" Morgan asked politely, wishing that she didn't have to deal with this.

"Listen, I'm sorry. I know that I was rude and I shouldn't have been. I'm just very protective of Patrick. And, well," Aileen lifted her hands and let them drop, gesturing to Morgan, "you're just so beautiful and nobody knows your past. I wanted to know what you were about. So, I'm sorry."

Morgan felt the tension draining out of her shoulders and she smiled tentatively at Aileen.

"Thank you. Both for the apology and the compliment. I'm just really shy," Morgan said.

"So Mum said. I shouldn't have poked at your family stuff either. It can't have been easy growing up without a family."

"Aye, it wasn't. The hardest years of my life. Or so I hope. I'm okay with talking about the past, it's just that I'm trying to move forward. Build a life for myself." Morgan shrugged a shoulder, not sure how else to explain.

"And I admire that. I'd like to formally extend the offer of my friendship and I hope that you'll come have a drink at the pub with me one of these days," Aileen said, real warmth coming from her this time. Morgan could tell that her intent was pure so she returned her smile with one of her own.

"I'd like that. Truly."

"Good, now that that's settled, I brought some of my lace with me," Agatha said, raising a leather tote that she was carrying.

Morgan clapped her hands and smiled.

"Wonderful, I'd love to see what we could do. Bring them over here."

"I'm just going to look around," Aileen said and wandered towards a stack of black-and-white photographs.

Morgan nodded and turned her attention to where Agatha had laid her lace out in various piles.

"Doilies, placemats, napkins, and these…aren't these sweet?" Agatha said, holding up a pure white Christening bonnet with lace trim. Morgan felt her heart twist a bit about the thought of a baby wearing one as well as in admiration of her fine work.

"These are beautiful. What a fine gift. I'd like to buy one for Cait," Morgan said impulsively and then stopped herself from adding "and Keelin." Keelin's pregnancy news was still being kept quiet and Morgan wasn't going to be the one to let the cat out of the bag.

"If you'd like to wait until the baby is born, I can embroider his or her name or initials on it," Agatha offered.

"That'd be wonderful, thank you."

"So, do you really think these will sell in an art gallery?"

Morgan scanned the goods laid out before her and nodded.

"My only concern is how quickly can you make these? I suspect that they will sell very quickly."

Agatha blushed and smiled, a determined glint in her eyes.

"As fast as you need them. I can pay my girls to help too."

Morgan fingered the plastic wrapping surrounding one of the placemats.

"I'm glad that you wrapped these in plastic, but I think we could up the presentation a bit," she said, nibbling at her lip.

"I actually had the same thought and brought some ideas," Agatha said eagerly and pulled several rolls of ribbon from her tote. "What do you think about wrapping these around and then tying a handwritten card to it?"

Morgan studied the ribbon and then pulled one from the pile. It was a thick crème ribbon, with a lovely sheen that made it look luxe. Wrapping it around the placemat and tying it she studied it.

"With a sprig of dried flower," she decided.

"Oh! Perfect," Agatha gushed.

"Yes, this is the ribbon. Tie a card and a little sprig of flower or stick with it and it will be lovely and unique. I'll take them all. What will you sell them for? I was thinking a 50% commission but because you are local, I'd offer a 60% deal. We'll keep 40% of the profit and you keep the rest. Will that work for you?"

Agatha's mouth dropped open and she looked like a fish out of water gasping for air, before she clutched at Morgan's arm.

"Sixty percent? The stores in Dublin just buy them at a flat rate. I have no idea what they sell them for."

"Why that's just wrong. You're probably losing money. What do you sell say, four napkins for?" Morgan asked, her eyebrow raised. She was quite certain that Agatha was getting ripped off.

"Hmm, 4 euros a napkin. Twelve for the set?"

It was Morgan's turn to look like a fish out of water.

"Sure and you're giving me a heart attack. These are handmade! You must charge a premium for these," Morgan said.

"What should I charge? Oh, I don't even know," Agatha said, worry in her eyes.

"Told you that you were getting ripped off," Aileen called from across the gallery.

"I think if we package them nicely and have a little story about how they are made in the village, we could easily sell a set of these napkins for 34 to 40 euros," Morgan mused.

"You've got to be kidding me. For napkins?"

"You'd be amazed at what tourists spend their money on. And, a handmade local gift…they'll eat it right up."

"Why, we could take a nice vacation. I could pay my daughters to help, this could be wonderful," Agatha gushed.

"I think it will be perfect. We'll set up a lovely set of shelves to display your work," Morgan agreed and jumped when Agatha impulsively hugged her. She stiffened for a moment and then returned the hug, trying not to think what she had been doing with this woman's son the night before.

"Thank you. I don't know why I haven't tried to sell it locally before. I guess I just didn't think I was good enough," Agatha whispered.

Morgan pulled back and smiled down at her.

"Your work is truly art. It's an honor to have it in the shop."

"Aileen, I hope you're ready to work," Agatha called to Aileen as she turned to leave. "Come now, we must get started on the bows and labels. Let's stop by the flower shop for some of their dried blooms. It will be a lovely addition to the label. Bless you, Morgan!" Agatha called over her shoulder and Aileen waved as they swung out the door, their heads bowed together as they chatted animatedly, mother and daughter in synch together.

A part of Morgan wished for that same closeness.

She waved the brief spot of melancholy away and turned back to the pile of lace. And just like that, she'd added two more people to the group that she could call friends in this village.

It felt good, she decided. She was slowly putting down roots, making friends, even building a little network of support for herself.

She hadn't known how much she wanted it until she'd had it, Morgan thought as she stacked the piles of lace on a shelf in the back, wanting to wait to sell them until they had their labels.

Coming to Grace's Cove had been the best thing for her. She just wished that she could shake the feeling of imminent danger that crept up the back of her neck. Was it just because she had struggled for so long that she wasn't able to accept joy into her life? Morgan paused to consider the thought. This was a question for her session with Baird. Why was it that she felt like she was waiting for the other shoe to drop? As though she wasn't deserving of happiness, Morgan mused.

I am though, Morgan thought. *It's my turn. I'm going to hold on to this with all I can.*

The bells tinkled again and Morgan turned to greet her next customer, pushing her uneasiness aside. There was work to be done.

"Are those lace? Oh, how lovely," the customer said, looking at the lace doilies in Morgan's hand.

"They are. And made by an extremely talented local artist." Morgan smiled and calculated the sale in her head. She couldn't wait to tell Agatha.

Chapter Twenty-Five

THE REST OF the week passed in a blur of late night visits and early mornings. Morgan had even brought herself to stop at the pub for a cider after work one night. She'd been entertained with stories from the locals and had even accepted a dance with old Mr. Murphy. He'd kept her on her toes and had made her laugh when he blushed after she dropped a kiss on his cheek.

Slowly, the village seemed to be absorbing her and she it. She was excited to tell Fiona about her week, Morgan thought as she put a small package on the seat of her van before settling into the driver's seat.

"Come on, baby." Morgan sweet-talked the van as the engine struggled to catch and then let out a cheer as the engine roared to life. She made a mental note to get it to the mechanics one of these days.

As Morgan directed the sputtering van out of the village, she allowed her mind to daydream.

This week with Patrick had been like an awakening to her. Both physically and mentally. She found herself laughing more, craving his touch, wanting to tell him things through the day.

So why couldn't she shake this sense of impending doom? Morgan sighed as she looked out at the afternoon sun's rays that slashed across the sea-green water. By all accounts, her life was perfect.

Morgan pulled a sharp right onto the gravel lane that led up to Fiona's cottage. The van shuddered to a stop and Morgan smiled as Ronan came racing around the corner, his barks joyous.

"Hey, boy," Morgan said as she climbed down, the package in one hand. She scratched behind Ronan's ears and the dog immediately rolled over and exposed his stomach to her.

"No shame, huh, fella?" Morgan laughed and obediently scratched his tummy while he wiggled against the grass.

"Just in time, I've a lovely casserole about to be done," Fiona called from the open door and Morgan approached, smelling the scent of garlic on the air.

"Smells wonderful," she said and smiled at Fiona. The old woman's cheeks were flushed with heat from the oven and she came forward to hug Morgan. Morgan automatically stiffened but almost immediately relaxed. She was getting better at being touched, embracing people. It seemed like a way of life for the people of the village. They were always kissing each other and hugging goodbye quite casually. Morgan hoped that she would be comfortable with it all in a few more months.

"It's comfort food. I was in a mood," Fiona said and shrugged. Morgan tilted her head and really looked at Fiona. Though she smiled pleasantly, there seemed to be some tension around her eyes.

"What's wrong? Do you not feel well?"

Fiona laughed and waved for her to sit.

"Fit as a fiddle. I just feel like something is off. Or wrong." Fiona waved her hand again. "Probably just foolishness."

"Like an impending doom?" Morgan asked, her eyes trained on Fiona as the old woman pulled a steaming casserole from the oven.

"Aye, that'd be a good way to say it," Fiona said and sliced into the gooey mass of cheese and noodles.

"Me too. I have that feeling too!" Morgan exclaimed.

"You do? Oh, oh no. Now I am worried," Fiona murmured as she dished out heaping helpings of lasagna onto the waiting plates. Walking over to the table, Fiona deposited the piping-hot food in front of Morgan and then went back for the garlic bread. Sitting across from her, she raised an eyebrow at Morgan.

"Go on. Explain yourself."

Morgan immediately tore off a chunk of the steaming garlic bread as its scent was making her mouth water.

"I don't know. I honestly thought it was just me. Like, because things have been going really well for me. And, well, they never have before. I keep waiting for it to go wrong, I guess," Morgan said.

"You and Patrick?" Fiona asked as she took a bite.

"Yes, he's just...oh he's great. He's kind and funny, but not afraid to be the man. I feel like he really wants to be with me and take care of me. Even with all of my insecurities and bag of issues," Morgan laughed ruefully.

"You told him about your abilities, yes?" Fiona said, meeting her eyes.

"Well, most of them. Not the levitating stuff. Since I'm not going to use it anymore I figured he didn't need to know."

Fiona's hands stilled and she watched Morgan carefully.

"What do you mean that you won't be using it anymore?"

"Since you taught me to shut it off...I can. It's great," Morgan said enthusiastically.

"And what happens if it doesn't work? During a dream or something while you're sleeping next to him?" Fiona asked carefully.

"I...I hadn't thought of that. I just thought that I could keep it off."

"And so you might. But don't you think he deserves to know so that you don't give the poor man a heart attack?"

"But...what if he hates me?" Morgan asked, fear lacing her voice.

"What did he say about the rest of your abilities?"

"Nothing really. He said he was used to it with Cait and it was no big deal."

Fiona beamed.

"I've always said that Patrick was a fine lad," she said, taking a sip of her whiskey.

"He is. I guess I will tell him about the rest of it. It's not a big deal, really."

"Well, I mean it is. It's a very unique power. I suggest that you point out to him all of the positive uses of it," Fiona said.

Morgan thought about it as she took another bite of the lasagna, savoring the flavors in her mouth.

"Okay. I will tell him. Tonight or tomorrow, whenever I see him next."

"Good girl. Maybe that's what's giving us this feeling of doom. Because you haven't been fully honest with him," Fiona remarked.

Morgan considered it. Did she feel better making the decision not to hide anything from Patrick? Maybe so.

"Perhaps. I guess it isn't a big deal. It just seemed like a lot to lay on someone at once."

Fiona pointed a finger at her.

"Honesty is always the best way. In magick, in healing, in using your abilities, in life…"

"In using my abilities, what do you mean?" Morgan asked in confusion.

"Say you used your abilities for nefarious purposes. Well, the harm you caused would come back on you two-fold. If you use them for the greater good, no boomerang effect then," Fiona said simply.

Morgan covered her face with her hands and cursed softly.

"God, no wonder you try to find each of us. If we didn't know these things, something really bad could happen. I'm glad that I was too busy hiding to really explore what I could do with my powers."

Fiona regarded her gravely.

"I'm only grateful that more harm didn't befall you. But, now you're in a good place. And, you're one of mine. So, what's in the package?" Fiona said lightly, gesturing to the package Morgan had brought in.

Morgan allowed the warm pleasure of being called "one of Fiona's" wash through her as she reached for the package she had brought.

"I thought you'd like this," she said softly.

"A gift! What fun," Fiona said and unwrapped the present eagerly, not bothering to hide her joy in receiving a present.

"Oh, this is just lovely," Fiona breathed and unfolded a swatch of lace.

"It's a table runner. Or you could put it on a shelf with some candles on it or something," Morgan said.

"I love it," Fiona said, her eyes shining.

"Patrick's mum makes them. I'll be selling them in the store."

Fiona's smile widened. "Even better. I've always liked Agatha too. Good family there."

Morgan decided against filling her in on Aileen's attack on her. Seeing as how they had smoothed things over, it was probably best not to gossip in a small village.

"Yes, I'm quite taken with her. Though their family is large. It will take some getting used to."

"I suppose it will at that. You'll do just fine with them, Morgan. I have no worries about you." Fiona smiled and stood.

"Now, fill me in on any gossip you've overheard at the gallery."

Hours later, Morgan was smiling as she opened the creaky door of her van and climbed up onto the seat.

"Come on, girl, you've got this," she murmured to it as the engine chugged over again. Her night with Fiona had been just right. Good food, great company, and a dog to curl up at her feet. She could happily do this every Friday night, Morgan thought. Though she knew that made her different than other girls her age, Morgan figured that she was making up for lost time.

"Thank you!" Morgan sang out as the engine caught and she creakily backed down the driveway before turning onto the dark road. Her old headlights were the only light on the road here and she squinted into the dark as she made her way slowly along the ocean road.

Ireland wasn't known for its great roads and this one fit the bill. One lane, curvy, and difficult to navigate, Morgan began to wish that she had left earlier in the evening before the sun had set.

"Ah, well. Just go slow," Morgan murmured, and crept along the road. She tapped the accelerator lightly with her foot as she approached a hill.

Nothing happened.

"What?" Morgan asked, pressing harder onto the accelerator.

Nothing happened and the van began to decrease in speed.

"Shit," Morgan cursed and steered the van as far to the edge of the road as she could, the bushes screeching wildly as their branches scraped the side of the van. Morgan turned the key off and then the lights, not sure if she should conserve the battery.

"Shit," Morgan said again, thinking about what she should do.

She was about seven miles from Fiona's house and easily another fifteen or so from the village. As the darkness crept in around her, Morgan tried not to panic. Taking another deep breath, Morgan opened the door and stepped out. The sound of waves crashing against the rocks below reminded her of her precarious position.

It really was dark out here, she thought as she began to walk a little bit to see what was around the next curve. The moon was a small sliver in the sky, casting the faintest of light for her to see by. At the top of the hill, Morgan scanned desperately for any light, or any cars advancing.

Darkness greeted her.

Panic skittered up her spine and she began to breathe slowly, forcing herself to calm down. If worse came to worst, she'd walk the seven or so miles back to Fiona's. It would just take a little longer navigating in the dark, she thought. Morgan turned and headed back down the hill and was just at her van when she remembered her cell phone.

"My phone!" Shaking her head at herself, Morgan opened the driver's door and dove into her purse, digging around in the contents to find her slim cell phone.

"Please be charged," she prayed, knowing that she had a tendency to forget about her phone as she rarely used it.

Finding her phone, she swiped the screen and saw that she had 20% battery life left.

"Yes!"

Scanning through her contacts, she thought about the time. Patrick would be at work by now, so it was pointless to call him. Morgan's eyes landed on Flynn's name. His spread was just over the ridge from Fiona's and Morgan knew that he might have the necessary equipment to tow her vehicle.

Praying again, she selected Flynn's name and then did a fist pump when she heard the ring through the tiny speaker.

"Hello? Morgan?" Keelin's voice reached her through the speaker. Morgan's heart sank. She couldn't call a pregnant woman out to tow her vehicle.

"Hey, Keelin, how are you?" Morgan asked politely.

"Morgan, what's wrong?" Keelin asked.

"Um, well, it's no big deal, I can call someone else," Morgan began.

"Spit it out, Morgan," Keelin ordered.

"My van broke down. I'm about seven-eight miles towards the village on the ocean road coming from Fiona's. I was wondering if maybe Flynn would be able to..." Morgan pulled the phone away from her ear. Keelin had cut her off with a single "On our way."

"Okay then. Okay." Morgan breathed out and wiped sweaty palms on her jeans. Now, all she had to do was wait.

Reasoning that she would be safer in the van, Morgan climbed into the row of seats in the middle and buckled up. If anyone whipped around either curve, they could smash into her van from either end. The middle was fairly safe, she concluded.

Morgan looked at her phone again, her finger hovering over Patrick's name. They'd texted a few times this week and it always surprised her to see something sweet from him on her phone. Deciding again not to bother him,

Morgan turned off her phone to conserve the battery and tucked it back in her purse.

The moments crept by incredibly slowly as she sat, alone in the dark, on the edge of the cliff and waited. She commended herself on not having a freak-out and for steering the van to the side of the road as quickly as she had. She could only hope that the mechanic bill wasn't huge.

Sighing, Morgan jumped as a light sliced across her rearview mirror. Praying that it was Flynn, she craned her neck to see the haze of headlights working their way along the curvy road behind her.

"Phew, that was quick," Morgan said out loud. In a matter of moments, Flynn's huge truck had reached her van. Thankfully, Flynn kept his lights on as he got out of the truck. Morgan bounded out of the van.

"Oh, thank you! I'm so sorry to bother you."

The passenger door cracked open and Keelin slid out. Morgan smiled at her, happy she was there, even though she felt bad for putting her out. Keelin looked lovely in her burgundy sweater that barely revealed the smallest of curves at her waist.

Flynn and Keelin came to stand in front of her, Flynn's arm automatically going around Keelin.

"What happened?"

"I don't know. I've been having some trouble starting it. But then as I approached the hill, the accelerator stopped working. I just pulled the van as far to the side of the road as I could and then it conked out."

"Were you at Fiona's?" Keelin asked, reaching out to pull Morgan into a quick hug.

"I was. I've never driven these roads back so late before; I suppose I should have left earlier."

"I doubt that would have made a difference with your car troubles," Flynn said. He walked around to look at the front of the van, figuring out how to open the hood.

"I'm going to have to tow it. I'll need a few minutes to figure this out," he called, pulling a flashlight from his back pocket and stretching out on the pavement to look under the front of the van.

"How is he going to manage towing it on this small road?" Morgan wondered.

"Flynn never ceases to amaze me. He is one of the most capable men that I have ever met," Keelin said, love and affection shining through her voice.

Morgan turned to her.

"How are you feeling?"

"Ah, so you know," Keelin said and smiled at her.

Morgan shrugged and nodded. "I'm sorry if you aren't talking about it."

"It's fine. I figured you would pick up on it at some point. I'll tell people soon enough. It's just been fun to have this little secret to ourselves for a bit, you know?"

Morgan nodded though she very clearly didn't know.

Out of the corner of her eye, Morgan caught light cresting the hill.

"Flynn! Car!" Morgan shouted, worried that he would be hit.

Flynn rolled quickly to the side and stood against the side of the van, pressed to the hill.

A car crested over the hill and Morgan held her hands up to block the light, while simultaneously waving her other arm to warn the driver.

The car came to a stop before it reached her van.

Morgan knew that car.

She groaned as Patrick stepped out, his face murderous.

"Uh oh," whispered Keelin.

"How did he know?" Morgan said.

"Flynn must have called him while I was in the toilet," Keelin murmured. They watched as Patrick approached Flynn and they talked for a moment. Turning, he stalked across the pavement until he reached Keelin and Morgan.

"Keelin," he said quietly, not looking at her.

"Hey, Patrick, oh, I think Flynn needs…" Her voice trailed off as she stepped away, leaving Morgan in the line of fire.

"Get in my car," Patrick ordered.

"But, I need to..."

"I said. Get. In. My. Car," Patrick bit out and Morgan's back went up. She shoved around him and stalked to the van to pull her purse from the driver's seat. Flynn stood at the front of the van.

"Do you need help?"

"No, I can do this. The fewer cars up here, the better. I'll call you in the morning," Flynn said, a small smile on his face.

"Thank you. The key's in the ignition. I owe you," Morgan promised, her cheeks burning in embarrassment at the scene that Patrick was causing in front of her now part-time employer. She stomped across the pavement and slid into the passenger seat, anger churning in her stomach.

Patrick slid in behind the wheel and carefully eased his car past the van and Flynn's truck.

"You're going the wrong way," Morgan said, her nose in the air.

"I'm going to take the inland route so Flynn can get started hooking your van up, if you must know," Patrick bit out, staring into the darkness.

Morgan crossed her arms across her chest, angry at Patrick, mad about her van, and not even knowing why she was so mad.

"You didn't have to make a scene in front of Flynn; he's my employer after all." Morgan turned to Patrick, glaring at him.

She could barely make out his face in the darkness, but she could see that his jaw was clenched tightly.

Silence descended upon them.

"Oh, the silent treatment? Lovely, just lovely. Real mature," Morgan spit out and turned her body away from him, praying the ride would go quickly. She didn't know what the big deal was or why he had come all the way out to be mad at her.

They sat in silence for the remainder of the drive, Morgan's anger building the closer they got to the village.

"What is your problem? It's not my fault that my van broke down!" Morgan finally shouted. Patrick pulled his car to the side of the road, slamming on the brakes and causing Morgan to jerk against her seatbelt.

"You are supposed to call me. Me! I'm your boyfriend. I'm the one who rescues you!" Patrick yelled at her, a vein sticking out in his head as he did.

"You were at work!" Morgan shouted right back.

"Then I leave work!" Patrick shouted.

"You can't just leave work," Morgan said in shock.

"I can. When my girlfriend is in an emergency, I most certainly can. You're stranded on a dangerous road in the dark and you call Flynn. Not me. Flynn," Patrick said, biting out the words.

"I didn't realize I was your girlfriend," Morgan said snarkily, latching on to anything she could to fight back, caught up in the moment.

Patrick stared at her, his mouth dropping open. Closing it, he started the car, pulling back onto the road in silence and driving directly to her apartment building. Morgan sat in silence, feeling guilty, but also feeling righteous. They'd never discussed what they were to each other. There was no contract that said the girl had to call the boy when she was in trouble, she fumed to herself.

Patrick stopped the car, his eyes shooting daggers as he gestured for her to get out.

"If this week has meant nothing to you, then fine, we can just be friends."

Morgan's mouth dropped open.

"I never said this week didn't mean anything to me. I just didn't realize that I was supposed to call you first," she began.

"Save it, Morgan. You are too strong to ask for help, is that it? Always going it on your own? You don't need anyone? Fine, then. Just fine. I'll see you when I see you," Patrick bit out.

Ice washed over her heart and Morgan stumbled from the car, unable to speak, unsure what had just happened but knowing that she felt like she was going to be sick. She shoved the key in the lock and ran up the steps to her apartment, tears blurring her vision. On a sob, she rushed to her bed and fell facedown on it, her heart cracking open.

She never should have given her heart away, Morgan thought. Hadn't she learned by now? Her body shook as she pulled the covers over her head, willing the pain to go away. So, maybe she'd made a mistake by not calling Patrick. But it wasn't like she'd offended his honor or something. She'd been looking out for him and his work, Morgan thought angrily as she punched the pillow beneath her face. And, he sure had never asked her to be his girlfriend, had he?

Morgan felt guilt wash over her as she thought about what she had said. Patrick had taken her to meet his family. When she freaked out, he'd patiently listened. He had also very tenderly and very sweetly shown her what intimacy was.

Morgan groaned again and looked at her watch. The pub would be in high swing now with the annual boat races tomorrow. Patrick would have no time to talk and it was best she waited until morning. He'd work off his mad a bit and then she could apologize.

Resolved, Morgan turned and stared at the ceiling, waiting for sleep to claim her.

Chapter Twenty-Six

THE NEXT MORNING, Morgan paced in front of her slow pour-over coffeemaker. She'd spent a restless night, continually getting up to see if Patrick had texted her. Finally, at three in the morning, she had sent him a text saying that she was sorry.

Morgan sniffed and put her nose in the air. He'd certainly never bothered to respond. Probably laid up with some girl right now, Morgan thought and then pushed the thought away. Patrick may have a fine Irish temper but she didn't think he would do something like that to her.

At least she hoped he wouldn't.

Sighing, Morgan brought her cup of coffee to her face and inhaled the scent, sipping the liquid fast even thought it burnt the roof of her mouth. She had just enough time to hop in the shower and get ready before she would meet up with Aislinn.

Today should be fun, Morgan thought as she dipped her head under the warm stream of water, reveling in the calm that showers always seemed to bring to her. She wondered when she would see Patrick and if he would still be mad at her.

Morgan reached out and snagged her coffee cup from the sink, drinking the rest of it in the shower. Finally conceding that she had to get ready, she got out and dried off. Wrapped in a towel, Morgan went to her window to peek out at the weather.

Sunshine greeted her and Morgan smiled at the strings of flags that crisscrossed across the street down to the harbor. The town sure did know how to make a festive event. Feeling a bit better about her morning, she went to her closet and pulled on jeans and a bright pink shirt, finishing it off with a turquoise scarf tied around her neck. She let her hair air dry in loose waves down her back.

Sure and didn't she have the worst dark circles under her eyes, Morgan thought as she examined her face in the mirror. Pulling out her concealer, she went to work on her face, adding some color to her cheeks and a dash of shadow at her eyes. She'd probably just wear her sunglasses all day, Morgan thought and went to where a plastic shopping bag from last weekend sat on her small side table. Inside was a pair of new black sunnies that had caught Morgan's eye. She slipped them on and checked herself in the mirror again. In her opinion, she didn't look like a girl who had been up crying all night over her boyfriend.

Boyfriend. Morgan turned the word around in her head as she pounded down the stairs, pulling the door of her apartment open to step into the sun. She supposed Patrick was her boyfriend. They'd just never talked about it. Didn't he know that she needed to talk about things? She'd never done this before. Why couldn't Patrick see that she needed these steps in their relationship? Feeling her anxiety kick up a notch, Morgan pushed Patrick from her head as she made her way to the gallery where she was meeting Aislinn.

Cheerful streamers crisscrossed across the street, making the colorful town appear even more celebratory. The sidewalks were crowded with people laughing and already sharing their first pint of the day. Morgan shook her head at them, knowing they'd be in for some pain tomorrow if they drank all day.

Morgan could already see the harbor filling up with people as they walked past the street vendors parked by the boardwalk and called out to people on their boats. It was the official kickoff to spring and people were happy to be out in the sun.

Slipping down the side street that led to the alleyway behind Wild Soul Gallery, Morgan pulled her phone from her pocket to check for text messages. Her heart jumped at the blinking light and she swiped the screen to see the text.

From Flynn.

Morgan sighed and read that her van needed some work and he'd take it into the mechanic this Monday. Shooting off a grateful text, she pushed down the worry that came from not having heard from Patrick. Laughter floated over the fence around the courtyard behind Wild Soul Gallery as Morgan pushed the gate open.

"Morgan!"

Morgan stopped. Her heart filled with light as she looked at the beautiful group of women sitting around the table in the courtyard. It was almost as if they were surrounded by a glow of love. Aislinn looked every inch the artist with her wild curls twisted back from her face and a long skirt in a vibrant sea green brushing feet clad in jeweled sandals. Cait was glowing in a pair of maternity jeans and a bright white maternity top that had thin stripes crisscrossing it. Keelin grinned at her, the hunter green top she wore highlighting her pretty burgundy eyes.

"Fiona!" Morgan said, seeing the old women tucked behind Keelin, wearing a bright shawl in a mix of greens and blues.

"Of course I wouldn't miss the boat races," Fiona said with a smile.

"We're all here," Keelin said, and the women jumped as Keelin wiped tears from her eyes. "Sorry, sorry, just hormones."

Fiona patted Keelin's hand lightly.

"It's good to get emotional about this stuff. My girls. All together. And each one of you a picture," Fiona said, turning to smile at them all. Morgan couldn't help but smile back, feeling her heart fill with love and light from this tremendous group of women before her. Aislinn reached out a hand and pulled her to her side, wrapping an arm around her.

"How'd things go with Patrick?" Keelin asked and the other women whipped their heads around to look at Morgan.

"What happened?"

Keelin filled them in quickly as Morgan tried to figure out what to say.

"We fought. It was bad. I said some mean stuff. He stormed off. I texted an apology last night, but he never responded." Morgan shrugged, trying to blow the whole thing off.

"Well, that's right stupid of him," Cait said furiously.

"No, it's fine. Let us figure this out, Cait," Morgan pleaded.

"Fine, but I can still think he's stupid," Cait grumbled.

"What was he really mad about, Morgan?" Aislinn asked.

Morgan sighed and sat at the table, propping her arms on it and resting her head in her hands.

"That I didn't call him when my van broke down. Like I need him to rescue me," she scoffed.

The women all simultaneously rolled their eyes.

"I told Flynn not to call him," Keelin said with a sigh.

They all collectively shook their heads in disgust at men.

"So that was what the fight was about?" Aislinn prodded.

"Yes. That and that he kept calling me his girlfriend. Saying that a girlfriend would have called him. I told him that I didn't realize he was my boyfriend and he blew his lid!" Morgan said indignantly, looking around at the women and waiting for them to agree with her.

"Ohhhh, hmm. Maybe he's not so stupid," Cait amended, slicing a glare at Morgan.

"What?" Morgan said, turning to Aislinn with her mouth open.

"Well, you see, it's just that you've been acting like you are in a relationship. And Patrick's mooned after you for months now. It probably hurt him a lot to hear you dismiss him like that," Aislinn said soothingly, running her hand over her arm.

"He never said! He never told me that's what we were!" Morgan said desperately, pleading her case.

"Alright, ladies, back off," Fiona said. "This is Morgan's first real relationship. Might I remind you about your first boyfriends, Cait and Aislinn?" Her steely gaze pinned each of the women and they both blushed, looking down at the ground and muttering.

"Sorry, Morgan. I get it. First love is messy. You guys will work through," Cait said amenably.

"Everyone keeps saying first love! How do I even know if it's really love?" she asked.

"Did he make you so angry you wanted to scream but then you felt like throwing up when he walked away?" Keelin asked.

"Yes," Morgan whispered.

"Do you light up when you see him and look forward to telling him things?" Cait asked.

"Yes," Morgan whispered.

"Does it feel right…in here?" Keelin asked, placing her hands on her heart.

"Yes," Morgan whispered again.

"Then congratulations, my dear, welcome to your first love," Cait said wryly.

"You were a hot mess with yours," Aislinn said to Cait.

Cait immediately shot her nose in the air.

"I most certainly was not."

"Are you kidding me? You made him mixed tapes with Forever Love written across them." Aislinn burst out laughing as Cait blushed.

"Alright, girls, enough. Let's head down to the races," Fiona ordered and the women all stood as one.

Fiona came around and wrapped her arm through Morgan's, looking up with her kind, all-knowing eyes.

"You'll be just fine, my dear. Let it go for today and enjoy yourself."

"I think that I might be able to do that now. Thanks," Morgan said, feeling lighter. It helped to talk with friends about her problems. It was another new experience for her, and it felt normal. For once, she felt normal.

"Wait up," she called to the women ahead and they stopped, laughing and gesturing for her and Fiona to hurry up.

Chapter Twenty-Seven

"IT'S SO FESTIVE!" Morgan exclaimed as they made their way to the harbor. Musicians were set up in chairs right on the boardwalk, playing a lively lilting tune that made Morgan want to tap her feet. Children raced in packs, urging each other to go faster along the boardwalk. It was a cacophony of color and motion and Morgan found herself enjoying it, instead of shirking away from the crowd like she would have in the past. She'd never been much of a joiner and it made her feel good to walk into this beautiful chaos of fun with the women at her side.

"Cider anyone?" Keelin asked.

"I'll have one," Morgan said impulsively. She could see Cait considering it.

Fiona nodded at Cait.

"You're due any moment. A cider won't harm the babe."

Cait grinned and nodded at Keelin.

"None for you though, Keelin," Fiona said and Keelin's face fell.

"I know, I know," she grumbled.

"I'll go with her," Aislinn said.

Morgan found herself scanning the crowd, trying to catch a glimpse of Patrick's tall frame.

"He's on Flynn's boat," Cait said dryly and Morgan jumped.

"I wasn't looking for him," she protested and then remembered who she was talking to.

"Uh huh," Cait said, but with a smile to take the bite out of her words.

Morgan found herself hypnotized by the sight of Patrick as he worked at tying flags to Flynn's racing boat. His arm muscles rippled as he moved and she sighed just watching him.

"You'll work it out," Fiona murmured at her side and Morgan tore herself away from looking at him.

"Cider!" Keelin called as she came back with a bottle of Bulmer's for Morgan.

"Thanks," Morgan said, lifting the bottle and taking a long pull from it. She stopped and then glanced at the girls. "Um, I'm going to need food."

"Fresh scones right there," Aislinn said, gesturing to a booth.

"I'll come with, I'm always hungry," Cait grumbled and meandered with her to the booth where they both purchased cinnamon raisin scones with sweet cream. They perched on a low wall to eat.

"This is nice," Morgan said, gesturing to the festivity around them.

"It is. The pub will be hopping later, so good for business."

"Where's Shane?" Morgan asked.

"The men are all going on Flynn's boat. Going to enjoy themselves a fast ride across the water," Cait said with a sigh.

"Envy them?"

"Aye, I love it. Whipping across the water with the wind in your hair and sun beating down on you…it's the best. You can't grow up on the water and not feel it in your bones," Cait said and bit into her scone.

"Do you think Patrick and I will be okay?" Morgan asked, her stomach still a ball of nerves at the possibility of losing him.

"Aye, he really does care about you. You'll work through this. Most couples I know have a good fight every now and again. It clears the air. And, making up is fun." Cait winked at her and then winced.

"What was that?" Morgan asked, alarmed.

"Just a twinge, nothing major. I suspect I'll be going later today or tomorrow," Cait said matter-of-factly.

"Oh God, what do you want me to do?" Morgan asked, jumping up and hovering over Cait. Cait laughed at her and waved her to sit.

"Nothing. Shane knows. And am I not sitting next to one of the greatest natural healers this world has known?" Cait gestured to where Fiona stood.

Immediately, the ball of nerves in her stomach soothed.

"I've never seen her work. What's it like?"

"It's an experience. I've only been with her once and quite by accident. It's almost like magic. You can see the sickness leaving too…almost like a blur of gray or a flash of light. It is enough to make you believe in pretty much anything," Cait mused, squinting at the harbor. "Ah, they're getting ready to go."

"Come on, girls," Aislinn called and Morgan turned, hauling Cait up by her hand.

"Promise me you'll tell me if you need help," Morgan whispered.

Cait waved her away.

"I'll be fine."

Chapter Twenty-Eight

The women picked their way through the crowd to where the entrance to Flynn's dock was roped off. One of Flynn's crew, and a man that Morgan had worked with before, nodding to them and held the rope up, allowing them front-row access to the boat races.

"Oh look!" Morgan cried and pointed to where Flynn's boat, decked out in flags and streamers, lined up next to ten other boats. Their men all ranged around the boat in varying positions. Morgan jumped as Cait let out a wolf whistle that had all the men turning. They waved as their ladies cheered for them.

Morgan felt her heart lift when Patrick waved. She waved back, hoping that he could see the smile on her face.

Hoping that he knew how much she cared about him.

The women linked arms as the announcer shouted over the loudspeaker.

"Five, four, three, two, one!" they all yelled together and began screaming like banshees at the end of the dock. The boats took off from the starting line, racing towards a boat far out in the ocean that Morgan could barely see. Flynn's boat was the easiest to track with the brightly colored streamers fluttering in the wind behind it.

"How far out is it?" Morgan asked.

"It's a mile out and back," Fiona said. "Nothing too bad. They'll move the boat in later so the smaller boats and sailboats can have a go at it."

Morgan squinted as the boats became tiny dots on the horizon while the crowd behind them screamed and cheered.

"What do they win?"

"Mostly bragging rights. And a nice championship cup that Flynn will likely be drinking out of later at the pub," Aislinn said.

Morgan watched as the tiny dots rounded the boat on the horizon.

"They're coming back."

The cheers increased in intensity and Morgan found herself caught up in the energy of the crowd as they all screamed for Flynn's boat to cross the finish line first.

"He's in front!" Keelin screamed and jumped up and down, waving her hands in the air.

"Yes! Yes!" Morgan found herself screaming as Flynn crossed the finish line first, the men in the boat jumping and cheering. The women exploded on the dock, screaming and laughing as they hugged each other and jumped up and down.

"Oh, oh I'm so glad they won." Morgan laughed, holding a hand to her pounding heart.

"This was the best race as all those boats have side bets. They talk it up in the pub for months before the race every year, threatening each other and betting against each other. It's great fun for them," Cait said, laughing and waving again at the boat.

"Who'd you bet on?" Morgan asked, knowing Cait.

"Flynn, of course."

Morgan laughed and watched as Flynn pulled his boat close to the others out in the water.

"Come on, ladies, they'll talk like that for a bit. I have to use the toilet," Cait said, pointing down at her belly. Fiona watched her carefully and nodded, signaling for the women to all go at once.

Morgan cast one last glance over her shoulder, her eyes searching for Patrick. He stood with his back to her, talking with a man on another boat. Sighing, Morgan followed the ladies down the dock, wanting to stay close to Cait.

Not that she knew how to heal, Morgan scoffed at herself. But, she'd help in any way that she could if Cait suddenly went into labor.

Morgan hurried to catch up with the women as they walked down the boardwalk to the road that led into town. She tensed for a moment as she saw them stop and talk to Agatha and the rest of Patrick's family. Aileen waved to her and Morgan forced herself to relax.

"Hi," Morgan said, coming to stand by Fiona's side.

"Morgan! Hello," Agatha said, giving Morgan a quick squeeze.

"Morgan gave me one of your table runners; I never knew that you did such exquisite work," Fiona said to Agatha.

"Your first sale," Morgan said shyly to Agatha.

"Morgan! You didn't have to do that. And, thank you, Fiona, I'm so glad that you like it."

"I suspect you'll be a wild success if you sell at Aislinn's gallery," Fiona observed.

"I certainly hope so. I have to say, I'm so excited! It's been years that I've been doing this in between looking after children. I'd be right happy to make a success of it now that I have all this free time."

"Here come the boys," Aileen said and they all turned to see Flynn leading the group of men down the dock.

Morgan felt her stomach twinge a bit. It sure was a fine-looking group.

"Lord and isn't that a handsome group of men," Fiona observed.

"Mmmhmm," the women all said in unison and then burst into laughter.

"I really need to use the toilet," Cait said, looking pained.

"Yes, let's go on up to the pub. We'll see the men there shortly," Fiona said briskly and the three of them began to follow Cait who had started to hurry up the road.

"I'll be just a moment," Morgan called, glancing back to where the men were surrounded by villagers congratulating them. Patrick's family moved towards him so they all formed a huge ring of people around the men. She was hoping that she could get a moment with Patrick to congratulate him, to ease the dull ache that was stuck in her stomach.

And the feeling of impending doom hit Morgan so hard, she almost doubled over from it, wheezing in pain. She gasped, whipping her head around.

Further up the hill, a car, traveling much too fast for a town packed with festival-goers, pulled out onto the wrong side of the street.

A tourist, Morgan thought numbly, opening her mouth to scream.

The compact sedan clipped the front of a truck and Morgan watched in horror as the combination of speed and the leverage of the truck sent the car flying into the air.

Everything slowed for Morgan as she heard the screams around her, from her, everywhere, as the pounding of her heart amplified a thousand times in her ears.

The car seemed to hang suspended for an instant, before it came crashing down on Cait who had hurried ahead of the group to get to the restroom.

"Cait!" Morgan choked.

Fiona and Aislinn turned to her instantly and screamed, "Morgan!"

And everything froze.

Chapter Twenty-Nine

MORGAN FOUND HERSELF on her knees, choking on sobs, not understanding what was happening.

Fiona's body was frozen, with her arm outstretched to Morgan, pleading with her to do something. Keelin was kneeling by the car where Cait's upper body stuck out from the fender. A pool of blood shone wetly around Cait's shoulders, the red bloodstains bright against the white of her shirt. Aislinn's face was frozen in a scream of terror as she stepped towards Cait and turned towards Morgan at the same time.

"What's happening?" Morgan screamed into the silence and the frozen bodies, her eyes unable to move from Cait's fallen form.

Morgan stood up and whirled, seeing the faces of the villagers, of the men. Shane's face was crushed in absolute devastation. It hurt for her to even look at him. And Patrick…her heart twisted and she tried to move forward but bumped into a wall of sorts.

"Help me! Somebody help her. What is happening?" Morgan screamed, banging her fists against the clear wall that stopped her movement, tears coursing down her face. Her breath came in ragged gasps and she tried to think. If only she could just think, she could figure this out.

"What will you do, Morgan?" A voice like whiskey wrapped around her and Morgan straightened, a shiver running down her back.

"Mother?" Morgan asked, a part of her knowing it wasn't her mother in this time, but her mother from ages ago. She turned.

Grace O'Malley stood before her, looking coolly lovely in a regal dress of red and gold, her dark hair curling wildly around her head, thick jewels at her throat. She was every inch the Warrior Queen and her eyes pierced Morgan with a fierceness that she felt to her very core.

"Stop this. You did this to her! Make it better. Take it back," Morgan pleaded, her anger ripping through her.

Grace drew herself up and scoffed at Morgan.

"I most certainly did not do this. You think that I would hurt one of my own?"

Morgan froze, anger from this life and lives past building deep in her core.

"Yes. You hurt *me*," Morgan shrieked, anguish pouring from her. "You left me. You just left."

Morgan choked as she struggled to breathe through the emotion that wrapped her lungs, fear for Cait and anger at Grace making her struggle to function.

"I had to leave, child. It was my time. I've never stopped loving you. Just because I was gone from your life, it doesn't break that bond. I've followed your soul for centuries. I'll always love you. You are mine," Grace said simply, her beautiful eyes full of kindness and understanding.

A sweeping rush of love and light filled Morgan, and a heaviness lifted off her soul, for just a moment.

"Then what! What is this? Why did this happen?" Morgan panted out, wiping her tears away, her eyes drawn to where Cait lay pinned beneath the car, her face terrifyingly devoid of expression.

"I can't say why it happened. All I can tell you is that it is through my love that I'm able to give you this chance," Grace said as she swept her arm around to the frozen scene surrounding them.

"What chance? What do you mean?" Morgan begged, knowing that the longer she argued, the less time Cait probably had.

"Why for you to save her, of course. You can lift the car from her," Grace said simply.

Morgan looked at her in horror.

"But, I can't! Everyone's watching! The whole town will know about me." Morgan whirled to look at Patrick's handsome face, contorted in a silent scream. "Patrick will know. I didn't get a chance to tell him about me," she sobbed out, caught in indecision.

"What will happen if they find out?" Grace tilted her head, compassion crossing her strong face. She took Morgan's hand, their matching scars seeming to burn together. Heat pulsed against her palm.

"They'll hate me! They'll run me out of town. I'll be all alone again," Morgan sobbed.

"What if they don't?" Grace asked.

"But, I've never tried to lift something that heavy. What if I'm not strong enough? If I can't do it, Cait will die!" Morgan protested, caught in the weight of her fears, insecurity ratcheting through her.

"She'll die if you don't," Grace said, her words slapping Morgan in the face.

Morgan straightened and looked around at the people frozen in various states of shock and horror. This was a village who cared about their own, she thought, as tears ran down her face. They'd accepted Fiona without too much fuss, and many knew of the rest. Cait was a town favorite.

"Love can win, can't it?" Morgan whispered, turning to face Grace, her heart in her eyes.

"Yes, my sweet, beautiful child," Grace said gently.

She took Morgan's face in her hands and looked down at her. "Maeve. Morgan. Two incredibly strong and very different women, both housing the same soul. We're forever bound, you and I. You're never alone. My blood runs in your veins. My love, my strength, is yours. Love always wins," Grace said as she placed a kiss on Morgan's cheek and faded away.

Like a bolt of lightening, Morgan was back on her knees in the grass as people screamed in terror around her.

"Morgan! Save her," Fiona shouted at her, her voice raw with fear. Aislinn whipped her head around as she ran blindly towards Cait.

"Lift the car," she screamed at Morgan.

And so Morgan stood, her back straight, her hands in fists at her side. She began to walk slowly towards where Cait lay pinned, her life's blood flowing from her, and she imagined that big switch in her head flipping to on with more power than she'd ever had in her life.

Pandemonium erupted when the car began to shift on its own. Wobbling at first, rocking a little.

Fiona and Aislinn had reached where Keelin kneeled next to Cait's head. They all turned to Morgan, their faces grim.

"Do it!" Keelin screamed.

Morgan continued to walk forward, and the crowd fell away. The noise seemed to fade into the background as she focused harder than she ever had in her life.

The car lifted straight off of Cait, hovering above all of the women. The crowd fell quiet behind her, only the scream of a small child resonating with her.

"I can't take my eyes off of it! Where can I put it?" Morgan screamed, wanting to move the car from over the women's heads, but convinced if she broke her gaze away, the car would fall again, this time crushing them all.

A voice cut into the silence behind her.

"Up the hill, Morgan, just up the hill two car lengths. It's free there."

Patrick.

Morgan tried not to let tears blur her vision as she held the car and slowly moved it through the air as it wobbled dangerously over the women. She followed it with her eyes until it hovered above a clear space.

And let it down ever so gently.

A sob escaped Morgan as she began to run, never looking back, only focused on Cait.

"Oh God, oh, no, oh," Morgan sobbed as she knelt in a pool of blood around an ashen Cait.

"Take the baby," Fiona ordered, her hands already on Cait's body, Keelin following her lead. Aislinn had her hands at Cait's heart, her eyes closed, her body still.

"What do you mean take the baby?" Morgan shouted.

Fiona whipped her head around to glare at Morgan.

"The baby is in distress. She knows her mother is injured. You need to tell her it will be okay and hold her steady until we get Cait back," Fiona bit out and Morgan stared at her blindly, more terrified than she had ever been in her life.

"Nooooo." A keening wail broke through and Morgan glanced up in time to see Flynn and Baird holding Shane off of Cait.

"Let them work," Flynn shouted into his ear.

"The baby!" Fiona ordered and Morgan whipped her eyes back to Cait's body. Ignoring everything else, she slipped her hands beneath Cait's shirt, sticky with blood, and pressed her fingers onto her swollen stomach. Closing her eyes, she scanned Cait's womb until she found a very frantic flicker of life.

"Shh." Morgan communicated with her mind. "It will be okay."

"My mother!" the baby cried to her, its screams of fear echoing in her head.

"We've got her. You need to calm down right now or you'll make it worse," Morgan said sternly and then winced, hoping that she hadn't scared the baby.

The flickering seemed to slow a bit and soon Morgan could sense a regular heartbeat.

"That's a good girl. We all love you and your mother very much. We are taking care of her. You'll be able to see her soon," Morgan promised the baby and she saw a warm glow begin to surround the baby as she spoke.

"You're doing good, Morgan, keep holding her. Cait's lost a lot of blood. Both of their lives are in danger," Fiona said curtly.

Morgan gulped and nodded, talking to the baby with her mind.

"Your mom is one of the best women I know. You'll grow up to be just like her. You'll love this town where you are going to grow up. It's located on the water and has all sorts of wonderful things to see and do," Morgan babbled, pouring all of her energy and love into Cait's womb, visualizing a cocoon of light surrounding the baby.

Morgan was dimly aware of Fiona and Aislinn chanting while they ran their hands over Cait, sweat pouring off their brows. Fiona's body shook with emotion and power as they held their hands to the worst of Cait's wounds. A hum of energy began to surround the woman as they worked over Cait's body, each woman doing her part to save one of their own.

"Hold on, little one, just hold on until I tell you it's time, okay?"

A small voice reached her mind again.

"Yes," the baby said simply, seeming to enjoy the cradle of light Morgan held her in.

A flash of light shot past Morgan's face and she whipped her head back, narrowly missing the stream. It shot into the chimney of a nearby house, exploding it in a fantastic display of bricks flying into the backyard.

Cait moved beneath them, moaning.

"We need to get her inside. This baby's coming," Fiona warned, looking ashen, her brow covered in sweat.

"She'll hold. She told me she would," Morgan whispered, refusing to break her tenuous hold on the baby.

"Lift her. Men, help!" Aislinn cried and in seconds Shane was cradling Cait under her arms while Patrick and Flynn lifted her feet. Baird hovered behind them looking anxious.

"To my house," Aislinn ordered and the men began to trot up the street. Morgan ran with them, her hands never leaving Cait's belly.

"Don't let my hands leave her belly," Morgan barked out, her eyes briefly meeting Patrick's before she returned to Cait's stomach.

"We won't," Shane said fiercely.

They maneuvered themselves awkwardly up the hill towards Aislinn's house next to the gallery. Baird ran ahead and opened the door, ushering them inside.

"First floor guest bedroom. Back left," he ordered and they followed him down a hallway. Morgan felt a picture slide off the wall as her elbow hit and she could only hope it wasn't an invaluable piece of art as it fell to the floor.

"Boil water," Fiona shouted behind them and Morgan saw Aislinn zip off towards the kitchen.

They entered a room with a beautiful bed with a wrought-iron bedframe and a wedding ring quilt on it, and Morgan tore her eyes away from Cait for a second.

"Move the quilt," she ordered and Baird snagged the quilt from the bed, throwing it over a rocking chair in the corner.

The baby sent a panicked cry to her brain.

"It's okay," Morgan murmured, not caring if she looked crazy to the men. "Your mom won't leave you. She'll be okay," she crooned, urging the baby to hold on.

Fiona whisked into the room, a cup of liquid in her hand.

"Hold her head up," she ordered to Shane. Shane dutifully did as Cait blinked wearily, moaning quietly.

"Drink," Fiona ordered.

And Cait drank.

Moments later, Cait began to cough, and then she began to cry.

Tears clouded Morgan's vision as Cait reached up with one arm and hooked it around Shane's neck, pulling him to her so she could kiss him.

"I hate to break this up, but you have some work to do," Fiona said gently, smiling through her tears.

Cait looked up at her, her face weary.

"I don't know if I can do it," Cait whispered.

"You can," Morgan interrupted, and Cait's gazed whipped to her.

"Your baby's fine. She, I mean it's ready." Morgan blushed, realizing that she had given it away. Cait began to laugh as Shane's mouth dropped open.

"A girl!" She sighed and smiled, her gaze returning to Fiona.

"You saved me," Cait whispered.

"Well, who was going to pour my pints for me?" Fiona asked, wiping a tear away.

"Free pints for life," Cait whispered and then worry crossed her face. "I feel so weak, I'm scared. It was so scary, everything that just happened, I saw the car, I thought…I thought I died." She hiccupped out a sob as Shane wrapped his arms around her again. The baby began to move in distress again, its heartbeat fluttering rapidly.

"Shh, you're fine. She's just a little emotional." Morgan spoke to Cait's stomach and had the woman pausing.

"Is she upset?" Cait whispered.

"She just got a little scared when you started reliving the moment. I think she's ready to meet you though." Morgan smiled gently at Cait.

"Will I be okay?" Cait looked at Fiona, her eyes wide with worry.

"Aye, you'll be fine. We're all here," Fiona said and Cait looked around. Morgan glanced up to see all of the women and their men standing around Cait's bed.

"Love wins," Morgan said.

"You're right," Cait said and Morgan jumped, not realizing she had said it out loud.

"Let's bring this baby girl into the world," Cait said and smiled, reaching to hold both Shane and Fiona's hands.

Morgan smiled and then sent all of her love to the baby, giving her a nudge in the right direction.

Chapter Thirty

MORGAN SLIPPED OUT as soon as she knew the baby would be delivered in good health. Aislinn's guest room was small and Morgan figured that Cait would want some private time with Fiona and Shane.

Her body felt like it had been run over by a truck and her eyes ached. She scanned the room, looking for Patrick.

"He went to man the pub. Everyone went there to wait and hear about Cait," Baird said.

Morgan nodded, not saying anything.

"You should go there," Baird said.

"I might," Morgan said noncommittally. She looked down at her bloodstained clothes. "I'd like to shower first. Give Cait and everyone my love. I'll…I'll be back," Morgan murmured, nodding at Baird as she tried to move past him.

"Morgan, if you need to talk...I'm here," Baird said gently.

"I just need to be alone," she whispered, at her emotional limit for the day, just needing a moment by herself to breathe.

Morgan slipped out of the back door and took the side streets to her apartment, jogging along so as not to chance running into a villager while she was exhausted and covered in blood. Morgan reached her apartment door and on a sob, she ran up the stairs to her room, jamming the key into her door, wanting more than anything to just be alone for a moment.

Pulling off her bloodstained clothes, Morgan pushed into the bathroom and stepped into the shower, not caring that the water was cold.

And let it all out.

She cried into the cold stream of water as it began to turn warm, slumping to the floor of the shower to let the water run from her. Pink water, the remnants of Cait's blood, flowed between her toes, getting sucked into the drain. Morgan wished she could wash away what had happened so easily.

Patrick hadn't stayed. He hadn't said a word to her, she thought as she tilted her head up into the stream of water.

And, yet.

He'd yelled to her. When she needed help most, Morgan thought. Her mind flashed back to the car hovering in the air and her fear of not being able to place it down safely. Patrick's voice had cut through her fear to help her.

Even when Patrick had been mad at her. Even when he didn't understand what was happening, he'd had her back, she thought.

That's just because he is kind hearted, and loves Cait, she told herself. If he really cared about her, he would have spoken to her after what had happened. Something.

An image flashed through Morgan's mind of the people surrounding her when she'd lifted the car.

Shock.

Horror.

Disbelief.

Morgan shook her head.

Nobody would ever look at her the same. And, they'd certainly judge Patrick for it. She'd always be known as his crazy girlfriend. She'd ruined everything, Morgan thought.

Realizing what she had to do, Morgan began to sob even harder, wrapping her arms around her legs, hating the decision that she had to make.

Morgan knew that she had to go.

Hours later, the tears still flowed as she packed her bags. Looking around at her apartment that she loved so much, her eyes landed on her bed. She trailed her hand over the comforter, remembering the nights that she and Patrick had spent there.

She was doing this for him, Morgan thought determinedly.

Her phone dinged with a text message and Morgan hurried over, hoping for good news.

Healthy baby girl! Cait wants you to come by tomorrow. She needs sleep now. Both mom and baby are doing well.

Morgan blinked down at the text message, happy that she had been able to help, grateful that Cait and the baby had been spared. Her body swayed as she looked at her phone and she realized that she was about to drop from sheer exhaustion.

She looked at her bed again.

"Tomorrow, I'll go," she said and crawled beneath the comforter, asleep before her head hit the pillow.

****

Morgan awoke in the dim light of morning to another ding from her phone. She pushed herself up and rubbed her hands over her face, trying to shake the fog from her brain. She closed one eye and squinted at the clock.

6:00 a.m.

Grumbling, Morgan reached for her phone to see who the text was from. Her thoughts immediately went to Patrick and her heart lifted for a second before she remembered that she was leaving today.

Sighing, Morgan swiped the screen.

I need you to open the gallery today. We have a tourist bus coming and Cait needs my help. Thanks, the text from Aislinn read.

Her mouth dropped open and Morgan began to text back, thinking up some excuse as to why she couldn't make it.

"Damn it," Morgan cursed and put the phone back down without sending a text.

She couldn't just walk out on Aislinn. She was the first person who had ever taken a chance on Morgan.

Sighing, she crawled back into bed and pulled the pillow over her head, pushing her nervousness away. She'd just have a heart-to-heart with Aislinn later on today and then she would be free to go.

On her own, once again.

Chapter Thirty-One

"WHAT AM I DOING," Morgan moaned as she finished getting ready for the day, her eyes drifting to her suitcases stacked in the corner. She sighed as she pulled her long hair into two braids on either side of her face, the mindless task soothing her. Her stomach growled, reminding her that she hadn't eaten since the scone for breakfast yesterday. Moving to the kitchen, she popped a piece of bread in the toaster oven and sipped at her coffee, trying to calm her scattered mind. Her emotions were raw and ran dangerously close to the surface. Morgan knew she would have to keep them buried if she was going to function at work today.

Morgan buttered her toast and bit in right away, barely tasting the food. Why hadn't Patrick called her? She must have scared him, Morgan thought, nerves skittering through her belly. Except he'd helped her. So why hadn't she heard from him? Morgan's thoughts continued to careen around her head in a cycle of insecurity and sadness as she grabbed her purse and her sunglasses and left her apartment.

Stepping into the sunshine of the early morning, Morgan caught sight of the cheerful flags that just yesterday had filled her with such excitement. Wanting to stay out of sight, she took the backstreets, wandering past people's kitchen windows, hearing the murmured discussions over breakfast. She dipped her head and kept her eyes on the ground, not wanting to speak with anyone.

Arriving at the courtyard to the gallery, Morgan couldn't help but glance at Aislinn's house. She wondered how Cait was doing. A part of her itched to see the baby that she had communicated with yesterday. Instead, she lifted the latch and went into the gallery, switching into work mode as she thought about what would be the best items to sell to the tourists. Morgan refused to think about the decision she had made.

Agatha had brought in her ribbons earlier this week so Morgan pulled a low table out from the store room and spent a good twenty minutes wrapping the ribbons around the packages, smiling at how cute they looked. She anticipated strong sales. Her smile dimmed a bit as she realized that she wouldn't be around to give Agatha the good news.

Glancing at the clock, Morgan realized that she couldn't put off opening any longer. With a heavy heart,

Morgan went and unlocked the door for what would possibly be her last day at the gallery. She pulled the shades, letting the morning sunlight slash through the windows to warm the honey-toned wood floors. She wandered around the room, her eyes taking in the beauty of Aislinn's painting, knowing that she would miss this place more than any other that she had left in her lifetime.

The bells over the front door tinkled, making her jump and a flush cross her face. Turning, she pasted a bright smile on her face.

Aileen stood there, a rose in her hand, a warm smile on her face.

"Aileen!" She was quite possibly the last person that Morgan had expected to see. A thread of nervousness slipped up her back.

"Morgan, I know our relationship got off to a bad start but I wanted to be the very first to thank you," Aileen said, coming to a stop in front of her and holding out the rose. Morgan looked at it in confusion.

"What. Why?"

"For saving Cait. We all love her. And I don't care how you did it, I just care that you did," Aileen said gently as Morgan took the flower from her.

Morgan blinked down at the single flower in her hand, the petals a pale yellow tinged with orange at the tips, so perfect in their unmarred beauty.

"You don't have to thank me," Morgan stuttered.

"We do. I do. You're a part of us now," Aileen said and then looked behind her at the door. "Listen, I have to go but let's grab a drink next week. I want to grill you about how you did the floating car thing."

Morgan laughed and impulsively reached out to hug the girl, still in shock over what she had said.

"See you later!" Aileen called and disappeared.

Morgan brushed her finger over the petals and smiled, looking around the room for a vase. Maybe everything would be okay, she thought. And for the first time since yesterday morning, hope filled her.

The bells tinkled and Morgan jumped, again turning with a smile.

"Mr. Murphy!" Morgan said and smiled at the gentleman who had given her a turn on the dance floor last week. In his hand he held a small bouquet of daisies. He came to stand in front of her with a smile.

"These are for you. Were my wife's favorites. Wanted to thank you for saving Cait," he said gruffly.

Morgan took the flowers and looked up at him, her heart shining in her eyes.

"You don't have to do…"

He cut her off with a wave as he turned to go.

"I give credit where credit's due."

And a moment later, he was gone, leaving Morgan to stare dumbly into her hands at the flowers.

The bells tinkled again.

"Agatha! And...wow," Morgan said as Patrick's entire family walked into the store, all holding flowers. His nephews, his sisters.

Everyone except for Patrick.

They filed past her in a stream of "Thank yous" as they handed her flowers. Morgan's arms were soon full and they were gone just as quickly as they had come. The door popped open again, and a woman she recognized as the grocer came in and deposited a flower on her already full stack with a friendly smile and a thank you. Morgan watched helplessly as one by one, the entire village came into the gallery, putting vases of flowers on the tables around her, piling them in her arms; it was like a flower shop had exploded in the gallery.

And her heart just sang.

By the end of it, Morgan was openly crying, unable to hold back the rush of emotion that came from being truly accepted for once in her life. What had she been thinking of when she wanted to leave this town? This was her home.

Morgan choked on a sob as Fiona walked through the door, her face wreathed in a smile.

"Smells lovely in here," she said softly, coming to a stop in front of Morgan and searching her eyes.

"Did you do this?" Morgan asked, gesturing with her arms full of flowers.

"I did not," Fiona said. "Besides, I was a little busy with Cait," she added with a small smile.

"Cait! How is she? How did it go? I should bring her some of these flowers," Morgan said immediately.

"Oh, she has plenty. Mr. McGuiness drove to the next town to buy out their flower store too," Fiona laughed and then reached up to run her hand down Morgan's cheek.

"My sweet girl, what a wonderful thing you did yesterday," she murmured.

"I was so scared," Morgan whispered, turning to lay the flowers down on the table. "God, I was terrified!"

"What happened to you? It was like your face went blank for a second," Fiona said.

"Grace froze time. I didn't even know that was possible. She told me…" Morgan hiccupped a sob and wiped her eyes again. "She told me our souls were bonded forever. And that if I didn't do anything, Cait would die. So, I had to save her. Even if it meant the villagers would run me out of town."

"Ah, she's quite the warrior, our Grace is," Fiona murmured.

"I didn't think that I could lift something so heavy," Morgan said. "I didn't know what was going to happen."

"Love will make you stronger," Fiona said.

Morgan nodded. "That's what Grace said. Love wins."

"You need to go see Cait. But first, there is someone waiting to speak with you in the courtyard," Fiona said, turning Morgan so she faced the back door.

"What? But what about the flowers?"

"I'll set about getting them sorted out. Will give me something to do. And, I'd like to give some to the driver of the car. Lucky woman, broken arm is all she suffered. Go on." Fiona waved, bending to scoop some flowers into her arms. Morgan stepped to the door, suddenly extremely nervous.

Trembling, she braced herself and opened the door.

Chapter Thirty-Two

PATRICK STOOD IN the courtyard, buckets of flowers surrounding him. When he saw her, his face creased in a smile and he slowly lowered to one knee.

Morgan gasped, and put her hand to her face, uncertain of what was happening. She slowly walked forward until she stood over him.

"I'm sorry that I didn't come to you. I'm sorry that we argued," Patrick said, his eyes shining with love and concern.

"It's okay, people fight, you don't have to kneel," Morgan said, reaching down to touch his arms, wanting him to get up.

"I saw what you did yesterday and..."

"I'm sorry that I didn't tell you. I'm so sorry," Morgan said, cutting him off and kneeling on the ground in front of him so they could look at each other as equals. "I shouldn't have kept that from you. I thought you would hate me."

Patrick raised an eyebrow at her.

"May I speak?"

Morgan found herself smiling.

"Sure," she said softly, her eyes searching his face, drinking in all of the details of his handsome features.

"What I was saying is that I saw what you did yesterday and, sure, I was shocked. But I was also amazed at your power. Look how amazing you are! So strong, so beautiful and that's when I knew," Patrick said and reached into his pocket.

"Knew what?" Morgan asked and then gasped as he pulled a ring from his pocket. "Patrick!"

"This isn't an engagement ring. I know we haven't known each other long and I know that we are young. But I was so proud of you yesterday and I saw how scared you were and I thought…this is who I want. I want to spend my life protecting her, making her feel wanted, loving her. I love you, Morgan and if you'll have it, I'd love to give you this promise ring," Patrick said, blowing out a breath, a question in his eyes.

"Oh, Patrick, yes. I'll take it, I love you too," she gushed, cradling his face in her hands, leaning into his kiss.

And everything fell into place for her, in that one singular moment. She could never leave this place, this man, Morgan thought as she sobbed against Patrick's lips.

She was home now.

Epilogue

MORGAN STARED DOWN at her ring finger, smiling happily at the gold band with a glint of ruby. Intricate Celtic designs were etched along the side. Morgan could feel the love resonating off it. She held up her hand, looking at Patrick.

"Whose was this? I can tell it was well-loved."

"Ah, Fiona's actually," Patrick said with a smile.

"Her wedding band?" Morgan said, her mouth dropping open.

"No, just a band that was given to her on an anniversary. My mum already had all her jewelry marked for her girls so I reached out to Fiona. I knew you two sort of had a bond going and she was more than happy to help," Patrick said with a shrug. "I would have bought you something but the jewelry stores were all closed."

"This is perfect," Morgan said, liking how the ring caught the light.

"Well, I knew that I needed to do something fast before you ran," Patrick said and had Morgan's head coming up.

"You knew I was going to run?" she whispered.

"Oh yeah, because that's what you do. That's why I had to put a ring on your finger to show you that you had a family if you wanted it," he said simply, smiling at her.

"Did you get the village to do the flower thing?" Morgan asked, leaning into his shoulder. His arm came around her and Morgan wanted to laugh from the sheer joy of being connected with someone.

"Nope: Mr. Murphy," Patrick said, smiling down at her.

"Mr. Murphy!"

"Well, everyone went to the pub afterwards and of course they were talking about what had happened. Mr. Murphy said we all owed you flowers and a thank you and they came up with the idea."

"So that's why Aislinn made me come to work today," Morgan mused.

"Tricked ya," Patrick said.

"Speaking of, I should go see Cait," Morgan said.

"Yes, I have strict orders to bring you over there," Patrick said, rising and pulling her up until they both stood, his arms around her as she leaned into him.

"Who will watch the shop?"

"Fiona locked it after her. Come on, let's go meet my new mini-boss," Patrick said and Morgan laughed at him.

Hand in hand they walked across the street to Aislinn's house. Fiona threw the door open before they got there and her eagle eye landed on the ring. A smile flashed across her face.

"Thank you," Morgan whispered, pulling her hand from Patrick's to hug Fiona.

"It was Maeve's," Fiona whispered in her ear and warmth flashed through Morgan.

"You'll make me cry again," she said.

"No tears, celebration time! I've been badgering Cait to tell me the baby's name but she hasn't yet," Fiona grumbled.

"Come on back," Cait called, still ensconced in Aislinn's guest room. Morgan followed Fiona back and they crowded into a room already packed with people. Aislinn and Keelin hovered over a small bassinet by the bed. Shane sat on the edge of the bed, his arm around his Cait, a dreamy smile on his face. Baird and Flynn chatted in the corner.

"Morgan!" Cait said, pleasure darting across her face. "It's about time."

"Sorry, I had a few things to do," Morgan said, glaring at Aislinn before breaking into laughter when Aislinn just smiled cheekily at her.

"Can I see her?" Morgan asked, nodding at the bassinet.

"Go ahead," Cait said with a smile.

Morgan tiptoed to the bassinet and her heart melted at the sight of a tiny baby with a shock of dark hair and the most perfect pink lips.

"You can hold her," Cait said and Morgan reached into the bassinet, careful to support her head, and cradled the baby against her chest.

The baby opened her blue eyes and smiled.

"She just smiled at me!"

"Probably gas," Shane quipped.

"No. It wasn't," Morgan said, smiling down at the baby who had recognized her voice.

"Well now that everyone is here," Cait said dramatically, "we would like to introduce you all to Fiona Morgan MacAuliffe."

Morgan almost dropped the baby.

"Woah there," Aislinn said gently and took the baby from her, smiling at Morgan over her downy head.

"Oh, that is just the sweetest thing," Fiona said, coming to the bed to kiss Cait on the cheek. Cait reached up to hook her arm around Fiona's neck to squeeze her.

"Are you sure?" Morgan said, her eyes glazed with tears.

"I heard what you did for me. I will never forget it. Nor will Fiona," Cait said, nodding at the small baby.

Morgan nodded, smiling through her tears, so happy she could burst.

Keelin threw up her hands.

"Great, now what am I going to name my baby?"

They all broke down in laughter and tears and Morgan passed her hand over the baby's head again, meeting Patrick's eyes across the bed.

"Hey, who won the bet?" Cait asked, looking up at Patrick.

Patrick's face looked thunderous for a second and then he sighed, a smile breaking through. He gestured to Shane.

Cait's mouth dropped open as she looked up at her husband. Shane patted his pocket smugly.

"Keeping the winnings in house, my love," he laughed down at Cait and she smiled.

"That'll teach you all to bet on me," she said smugly.

Morgan laughed again and settled into her new family, knowing that she could never leave this place.

Her home. Now and always.

Wild Irish Roots: Margaret & Sean

MARGARET TOOK A sip of her wine, watching Keelin dance her first dance as a married woman. How had she grown up so fast?

And somehow, Keelin had ended up back in Grace's Cove. The one place that Margaret had sworn she'd never go back to.

"Long time no see," Sean drawled from behind her and Margaret's back stiffened. Turning, she looked at Sean.

Damn, the man was as handsome as ever. The well-cut tux showcased his broad shoulders. Though a few grays peppered his hair, his presence still radiated strength and virility.

"Sean," Margaret said coolly.

"Come on, Maggie, that's the best you can do?" Sean asked, raising his eyebrow at her.

"It might be," she said, sticking her nose in the air at her nickname.

"I don't like that answer," Sean said, stepping closer and forcing her to look up at him. Margaret hadn't expected the punch of him. Heat licked low in her stomach.

"Well, you can't always get what you want," Margaret said flippantly.

"Yeah, so I've learned," Sean said bitterly. "But this time, I plan to."

Margaret's heart leapt into her throat as he pulled the wine glass from her hand and stepped closer, forcing her to step backwards into the darkness.

"What are you doing?"

"What I've been meaning to do for a long time," Sean said.

******

Watch for Wild Irish Roots: Margaret & Sean featuring the dramatic conclusion to Margaret and Sean's story.

To sign up for notification of a new release, please go here: http://eepurl.com/1LAiz

Please consider leaving a review! A book can live or die by the reviews alone. It means a lot to an author to receive reviews and I greatly appreciate it!

THE MYSTIC COVE SERIES

Wild Irish Roots

Wild Irish Heart

Wild Irish Eyes

Wild Irish Soul

Wild Irish Rebel

Wild Irish Roots: Margaret & Sean

Author's Note

On a warm, sunny day over a year ago, my husband and I hiked up The Saint's Path located on Mt. Brandon in Dingle, Ireland. The Stations of the Cross lined the path and led to the highest point of the peninsula. At the top, the winds were fierce and the view almost heartbreaking in its staunch beauty.

Days later, I awoke to the bells of the Christchurch Cathedral in Dublin, in a lovely hotel room. A dream tugged at my mind. So powerful, so insistent, that for the first time in my life, I was compelled to write my dream down, worried that I would lose the threads of the story that had captivated me in my sleep.

Over the last few days of our trip, I babbled incessantly to my ever-patient husband as he politely listened to me play with characters and plot.

Soon, my dream had expanded from one book into a five book series.

Sometimes, you just have to follow that moment. That brief hint of inspiration that lights you up inside. That…something…that keeps niggling at your brain. The Mystic Cove books are those stories. The ones that I think about when I'm doing yoga or in the yard playing with my dogs. The ones that make me ache to return to the shores of Dingle and spend many a day soaking up the beauty and charm that the small village has to offer.

Thank you for taking part in my world, I hope that you enjoy it.

Please consider leaving a review online. It helps other readers to take a chance on my stories.

As always, you can reach me at omalley.tricia@gmail.com or feel free to visit my website at triciaomalley.com.

You can sign up for new releases here http://eepurl.com/1LAiz.

Author's Acknowledgement

First, and foremost, I would like to thank my husband for his unending support as I pursue this wildly creative career of being an author. It isn't easy to watch someone follow the creative path, and uncertainties are rampant. Josh, thanks for being my rock.

I'd like to thank my family and friends for their constant support and all of my beta readers for their excellent feedback.

Thanks to Emily Nemchick for her excellent editing services and to Alchemy Book Covers for their stunning cover designs.

And last, but never least, my two constant companions as I struggle through words on my computer each day - Briggs and Blue.

Made in the USA
Middletown, DE
04 March 2017